*He stood behind her, her scent wrapping around him in a sensual cocoon, and he realised he was in serious trouble.*

The stance was too intimate, their bodies way too close. There was no way he could prevent his reaction to her as she wriggled to get into shooting position.

When her gun sagged in her hands, he clenched his teeth in frustration at their enforced proximity but reached around her to help hold the gun. "This time, don't close your eyes. It'll make it easier to see if you hit your target."

"How will I know if I'm on target?" Kelly demanded and he realised she was playing word games with him. He didn't know if he wanted to turn her around and kiss her or turn and walk away.

"You'll know."

She aimed again, and shot. And when the bullets rang out, she flung herself around in his arms, a pleased grin on her face. "I did it!"

"But you didn't hit anything."

"Not yet." And that's when she planted a kiss on Wade's lips.

# Available in July 2006 from Silhouette Intrigue

*Rocky Mountain Manhunt*
by Cassie Miles
*(Colorado Crime Consultants)*

*Denim Detective*
by Adrianne Lee
*(Cowboy Cops)*

*Out for Justice*
by Susan Kearney
*(Shotgun Sallys)*

*The Sedgwick Curse*
by Shawna Delacorte
*(Eclipse)*

# Out for Justice
# SUSAN KEARNEY

Silhouette and Colophon are registered trademarks of
Harlequin Books S.A., used under licence.

First published in Great Britain 2006
Silhouette Books, Eton House, 18-24 Paradise Road,
Richmond, Surrey TW9 1SR

© Harlequin Books S.A. 2004

Special thanks and acknowledgement are given to Susan Kearney
for her contribution to the Shotgun Sallys series.

Standard ISBN 0 373 22774 4
Promotional ISBN 0 373 60433 5

46-0706

Printed and bound in Spain
by Litografia Rosés S.A., Barcelona

## SUSAN KEARNEY

used to set herself on fire four times a day. Now she does something really hot—she writes romantic suspense. While she no longer performs her signature fire dive (she's taken up figure skating), she never runs out of ideas for characters and plots. A business graduate from the University of Michigan, Susan writes full-time. She resides in a small town outside Tampa, Florida, with her husband and children and a spoiled Boston terrier. Visit her at www.SusanKearney.com.

# CAST OF CHARACTERS

**Kelly McGovern**—The great-great-granddaughter of Shotgun Sally and Mustang Valley's most infamous citizen. Kelly is determined to pierce the veil of secrecy around her brother Andrew's death, even if it means moving in with the town's bad boy to protect her.

**Wade Lansing**—Mustang Valley's original bad boy and Andrew's best friend.

**Sheriff Ben Wilson**—Honest law enforcer or man with his own agenda?

**Jonathan Dixon**—A law school colleague of Andrew's with a chip on his shoulder and a grudge the size of Texas.

**Mayor Mickey Daniels**—He'll do almost anything to win his re-election—but does that include murder?

**Debbie West**—Andrew's fiancée and woman with a secret past.

**Niles Deagen**—Oilman extraordinaire or a man on the verge of bankruptcy?

**Lindsey Wellington**—New to Mustang Valley and Lambert & Church, she's determined to get to the bottom of Andrew's mysterious death, especially if it helps out her new friends Kelly and Cara.

**Cara Hamilton**—A fledgling reporter and Kelly's best friend.

**Andrew McGovern**—Kelly's brother lost his life much too soon. But was the fire that caused his death really an accident...or arson?

**Shotgun Sally**—The legendary frontierswoman influences the lives of Kelly, Lindsey and Cara in their quest for the truth!

For Phyllis and Sy Dresser

# Prologue

"Hi, short-stuff. What's up?" Andrew McGovern answered his sister, Kelly's, phone call with such enthusiasm that if she hadn't known better, she wouldn't have guessed he'd just worked an eighteen-hour day.

"It's after midnight," Kelly pointed out with sisterly affection. Andrew might amuse himself with his gadgets, like the caller ID that had told him she was on the line before he'd picked up the phone, but she'd bet her new diamond-bezel Rolex her parents had given her for a college graduation present that her brother hadn't checked the time in hours.

Papers rustled. She pictured Andrew behind his battered desk in the annex of his law office of Lambert & Church, his tie and jacket thrown over the back of a spare chair, his desk a mountain of papers, his file cabinet half-open, his eyes bleary despite the numerous cups of black coffee he'd drunk to keep him awake.

"And?" he asked.

"Don't you have anything better to do than work on Saturday night?"

''Nag. Nag. Nag.'' Andrew chuckled. ''Short-stuff, if you aren't careful, you'll start sounding just like Mom. And if, like her, you want to know if I'm still engaged to Debbie, I am. In fact, I'm bringing her to breakfast at the house tomorrow morning.''

Kelly sucked in her breath. Mom and Dad didn't approve of Debbie West's family and they certainly wouldn't be pleased about his engagement. Andrew's fiancée lived on an impoverished ranch just outside of Mustang Valley, Texas, about an hour north of town, with her alcoholic father and no-good brother. While Andrew seemed oblivious to his parents' reservations about his current relationship, Kelly's stomach knotted. She didn't like discord. Doing what her parents expected of her was so much easier than butting heads.

She'd always enjoyed her parents' approval, making straight As, being popular in school and avoiding trouble. Sure, sometimes she'd rather have been out partying than hitting the books on a regular basis, but she had discipline, something the brilliant Andrew, who often worked through the night but then didn't go into the office for another two days, knew nothing about. And she'd never understood why her older brother seemed so intent on riling up the folks by choosing friends from the other side of Mustang Valley. Like Andrew's best friend, that renegade Wade Lansing, who owned the Hit 'Em Again Saloon, and Debbie West, a high-school dropout who worked at a local diner.

Daddy had worked hard to buy the biggest house in Mustang Valley, and Mama had spent half her life decorating it. Kelly had enjoyed teen parties by the pool during high school and had been proud to bring home college friends to stay during vacations. Her best friend Cara Hamilton might not be as wealthy as the McGoverns, but she came from a middle-class home just a few streets away and now lived in a new apartment complex with nicely landscaped grounds and all the amenities, including a spa and security system. And she had a respectable career as a fledgling reporter. While her brother turned up his nose at the McGovern life-style, Kelly liked having her own horse and the pretty Jaguar Daddy had bought her after graduation. She saw nothing wrong with appreciating the finer things in life.

However, Andrew seemed to take pleasure in thumbing his nose at convention and the family. He hung out with whomever he pleased and rarely brought them home. Although he'd never been in serious trouble, Andrew had enjoyed racing his souped-up Mustang with dual chrome exhausts down Main Street and spying on the girls skinny-dipping at Half-Moon Lake. All harmless pranks— but ones that could have led to more serious trouble. Then, after finishing law school, instead of joining their father's oil company, he'd chosen to work at Lambert & Church, happily taking pro bono cases and mixing with all kinds of lowlifes, even criminals, as well as high-paying clients.

''Andrew! I think the only reason you date Debbie is to rile Mom and Dad.'' Kelly's older brother might hang out with some unusual people, but nevertheless the siblings were close. She enjoyed teasing him, especially about his friends. ''I thought

I should warn you…Dad still wants you to work for him. He's going to make you another offer.''

"I wish he wouldn't. I'm happy here. Busy. Needed." More papers rustled, and she suspected she had only half his attention. "In fact, I'm working on something real interesting."

His car alarm interrupted their conversation.

Andrew swore. "That stray cat must have jumped on my car, again, no doubt leaving sandy paw prints all over it, never mind waking everyone within a quarter-mile radius. Gotta go. See you tomorrow.''

"Bye." She set the phone back in its cradle with a shake of her head, turned off her light and pulled up her covers. She wouldn't have fallen asleep so easily if she'd known that was the last time she and her brother would ever speak.

# Chapter One

"Andrew's dead." Though Cara spoke to Kelly in her brash, no-nonsense reporter's voice, there was a catch in it. "And whatever you do isn't ever going to bring him back."

"I know." Kelly hugged her friend. If not for Cara's support, she didn't know how she would have made it through the past forty-two days. "Just hear me out."

"Okay." Cara plunked herself down on Kelly's bed, ran her fingers through her short red curls and stared at her through hazel eyes filled with concern and sorrow. A few years ago, Cara had been engaged to Andrew, but they'd mutually ended their relationship and remained friends.

Kelly tried to shove down her own grief over Andrew's death long enough to put her thoughts in order, thoughts that hadn't left her since the morning Andrew's body was found. "According to Sheriff Ben Wilson's report, an eyewitness saw Andrew chase the cat from his car, turn off his alarm and return to his office. But there was no witness to the fire that started in the annex of Lambert & Church sometime during the night.''

"Word is it was an electrical short, though the fire department is still investigating. Any reason you're suspicious it was something else?''

"Nothing concrete.'' But Kelly just couldn't let go. Not when the facts didn't add up. Kelly might have grown up the pampered princess of well-to-do parents, she might not have the bold brashness of Cara, but she had her own kind of genteel determination that had seen her through college and had left her with her pick of law schools.

She liked to believe that her toughness came to her from her grandmother's grandmother on her mother's side. Shotgun Sally had been a legend around this part of Texas for well over a century. Dozens of stories about her abounded, and one of Kelly's favorites was how the aristocratic-born widow lady had come out west at age twenty to start over and make a new life for herself and her sons. Now Kelly had suffered the loss of a dear family member—just like her famous ancestor. Somehow she would survive because surely a smidgen of Shotgun Sally's toughness ran in Kelly's blood.

Thoughtful, Kelly twisted a finger around a blond lock. "There was no witness to Andrew's death.'' A death probably from smoke inhalation since his badly burned body had been found still sitting in his chair. That he'd died in his sleep was little consolation to Kelly and her devastated parents.

Andrew might have been a rebel, but he'd been well loved. The entire town of Mustang Valley had turned out for his funeral and to pay their respects, including Debbie West, who'd arrived with her eyes red and swollen from crying. And Kelly had never seen Andrew's best friend, saloon owner Wade Lansing, so somber as when he acted as one of the pallbearers. Dressed in an immaculate black suit, shirt and tie that she wouldn't have suspected he owned, Wade had looked forbidding and dangerous, but had done Andrew proud, standing tall and strong beside her daddy, Sheriff Wilson, Mayor Daniels, and Donald Church and Paul Lambert, senior partners of the law firm where Andrew had worked.

Her father had tried and failed to remain stoic during the funeral, and he'd aged ten years in the past six weeks, his white hair thinning, the circles under his eyes darkening. Beneath her Vera Wang veil, her mother had wept copiously and Kelly should have been crying, too. But she couldn't. She was too angry at Andrew for dying. Too upset with the sheriff who couldn't give her any explanations why her brother hadn't even tried to get out of the first floor of a burning building.

Her world no longer made sense and she needed to put it in order before she could go on with her life. Finding answers for Andrew and herself might not be her specialty, but she was a fast learner and she fully intended to search for the truth.

''If someone else had been around, they would have gotten Andrew up and out of there.'' Cara's special brand of reporter logic made her good at figuring things out.

Kelly picked up a brush and ran it through her hair, not because her shoulder-length hair needed brushing but because she found the action soothing. "That night when I spoke to Andrew he was awake and excited. I have difficulty believing that he fell asleep so soundly that the smoke didn't wake him."

"The fire broke out at two in the morning. He must have been exhausted." Cara stood, took the brush from Kelly and tossed it on the marble and gold cosmetic table.

Kelly frowned at her. "Andrew was always the lightest of sleepers. Remember how picky he was about his sheets?"

"Huh?"

"Surely you haven't forgotten our sleep-over back in middle school when you put your puppy in Andrew's bed and she left a little sand behind."

Cara nodded with a chuckle. "Who would have thought a few grains of sand would keep Andrew tossing and turning all night? Or that he'd retaliate with an ice cold glass of water at 7 a.m."

"My brother required six pillows to sleep, propping up his knees and back. And now the sheriff expects me to believe that Andrew fell asleep in an uncomfortable office chair? It's just not possible."

Cara's eyes glimmered with interest. "*You* questioned Sheriff Wilson?"

Kelly shrugged. "Yeah. And he gave me a patronizing hug and told me he would look into my suspicions. Then I asked Paul Lambert what Andrew had been working on, and he just patted me on the head and told me the work was confidential. I don't know how you investigate your stories. People don't take me seriously."

"That's because you're…"

Kelly raised a perfectly arched brow. "What?"

"Polite."

"There's nothing wrong with good manners."

Except that six weeks after Andrew's death, Kelly had no more answers than she'd had the morning she'd been told he'd died. But she was determined to find out exactly what had happened that night. She just wasn't sure how to go about investigating.

However, Cara did know, and Kelly would eventually learn from her friend how to obtain the information she desired. Kelly might be polite but she knew how to get around Cara. "So you studied investigative journalism. Where should I start? What should I do? How should I act? What should I wear?"

Cara rubbed her forehead. "What if there's nothing to find? Can you live with that?"

Kelly stood, appreciating her height that allowed her to look down on her shorter friend. Andrew might have called Kelly short-stuff because she was a good eight inches shorter than his six-foot-two, but now she looked down her nose and used her most charming grin on Cara. "I just want to find out the truth. You of all people should understand."

"Of course I do, but… Look, Kelly. It's like this. While I was working for the high school newspaper on that exposé of the football coach and the school secretary, you were the head cheerleader. And in college—"

"Hey, I studied damn hard."

"I know you did, sweetie. Maybe you could investigate the society page or the travel section or—"

"Give advice to the rich and famous?"

"Exactly."

Kelly fisted her hands on her hips, careful not to wrinkle her silk blouse. "So you think all I can investigate is fluff?"

"If the hat fits…"

"…I'd wear it only if it were in style. But so what if I like fashion and gossip. That doesn't mean I didn't love my brother enough to find out what happened to him. Are you going to help me or not?"

Cara nodded. "I just don't want to see you hurt even more, but the last time I saw you this determined was the day you took your LSAT's." Cara looked her up and down, frowning at Kelly's elegant blouse and frilly, ladylike skirt that ended at midcalf. "I'd say a trip to the mall is our first stop."

"If anything happens to me, look after short-stuff." Andrew's words reverberated in Wade Lansing's mind as he walked down Main Street and spied Kelly McGovern.

Kelly looked different from the out-of-his-class woman that she always presented to the world. Instead of the feminine silk blouses and lacy skirts or designer dresses she favored, she was wearing jeans, boots and a tucked in blouse with a blazer. She'd done something to her standard shoulder-length blond hair, pulling it back softly with a clip that showed off her blue eyes and model cheekbones.

Wade wished he'd questioned Andrew more fully during the short phone conversation the night of his friend's death, but the bar had been packed and he'd been shy two waitresses. Still, he'd taken the time to ask Andrew why he thought anything might happen to him, but Andrew had told him it was probably nothing.

*Nothing, my ass.*

Andrew wasn't prone to panic or exaggeration. He'd stumbled onto something he shouldn't have and it had gotten him killed. And as much as Wade had liked and respected Andrew, his friend had grown up protected from the harsher side of life. Andrew trusted people, whereas Wade did not. Andrew always gave people the benefit of the doubt. Wade expected the worst, so he didn't need evidence to listen to his gut, which told him Andrew had been murdered. He'd been around trouble too many times not to trust his instincts.

As a kid, those instincts warned him to hide on Saturday nights so that his drunk father couldn't find him until he sobered up. The few times he'd forgotten to hide had taught Wade to never let down his guard. He had few friends, but Andrew had been a good one, and Wade owed him more than one favor.

Besides, watching Kelly's back and cute little bottom was certainly no hardship. With her long slender legs, she should wear jeans more often. She'd always been attractive in that don't-touch-me-I'm-off-limits-to-the-likes-of-you kind of way, which he'd accepted out of respect for Andrew. But today she actually looked approachable—if he could discount her five-hundred-dollar boots and the designer bag she'd slung over her saucy shoulder.

The sight of Kelly's new look not only reminded Wade of his promise to his friend but had his instincts screaming. He and Kelly didn't patronize the same kinds of establishments or reside in the same part of town. Kelly probably hung out in Dallas's or Fort Worth's fanciest malls or perhaps at Mustang Valley's finest steak house, but he'd rarely seen her on grounds he considered his turf. And why was she walking instead of driving her spiffy new Jag? What the hell was she up to?

His curiosity aroused, he followed her down Main Street past the post office and the pharmacy, keeping his distance and a few shoppers between them, considering possible destinations. Kelly didn't date guys from this side of town. She picked proper and preppie college boys with impeccable credentials and a family history as tony as her own. She'd only visited his saloon once to pull Andrew home during a family emergency. He recalled how out-of-place she'd looked in her lacy skirt and soft, sophisticated blouse, and yet she hadn't hesitated to enter his rowdy bar alone, shoulder past several inebriated cowboys to demand that her brother accompany her to the hospital. Her granddaddy had had a stroke. She'd looked sassy and sad then, letting neither Andrew's drunken state nor his lost cause of the moment, who'd been clinging to her brother's arm, deter Kelly from her task.

On the sidewalk in front of Wade, Kelly suddenly spun around and made a bee-line straight at him with that same determined pout of her lips that he so vividly remembered from years ago.

He braced for a confrontation. "Hey, short-stuff. What's up?"

"Don't call me that, please."

Kelly was always ultrapolite, but with him she usually sounded so irritated that she couldn't quite hide that annoyance. In return, he couldn't help feeling gratified that he was getting under that *Cosmo* girl skin. Maybe it was a remnant from his teenage years, but he loved bringing out the spark that she kept so carefully controlled. Watching her suppress all those simmering passions, he cocked one hand on his hip and pulled off her sunglasses.

She maintained a cool, superior tone, but vexation and perhaps a gleam of fury shined in her vivid baby-blues. "What are you doing?"

"I've missed your gorgeous green eyes," he teased.

"They're blue." She snatched back her sunglasses, her pretty polished pink nails shimmering in the sunlight. "Are you trying to distract me from the fact that you're following me?"

Ah, she might look like a fairy princess, even in those hip-hugging jeans, but she had a brain almost as sharp as Andrew's. Wade reminded himself not to get so caught up in the glisten of her lip gloss that he underestimated her. "You caught me in the act."

She chuckled, her lips absolutely adorable and way-too-appealingly kissable. "It wouldn't be the first time."

If she was trying to embarrass him with the memory of her walking up to the car her brother had lent him and her getting an eyeful of him and Mary Jo Lacy in the back seat, she wouldn't succeed. Of the three of them, she'd been the embarrassed one. Funny, he could barely recall Mary Jo's expression, but Kelly's had been a sight to behold. Her blush had started at her shapely chest, risen up her delicate neck, flowered over her cheeks and forehead. Her teenage-innocent eyes had widened in surprise before her lips had parted into a big round *O*.

"So what are you up to?" He eyed her from the tips of her new boots to the designer sunglasses she'd grabbed and thrust up high on her forehead.

"Nothing."

"Yeah, right. When I see Miss Kelly McGovern sashaying down Main Street on this side of town in blue jeans, I know something's up. If I didn't know you better, I'd think you had an assignation at the Lone Star Lodge."

"I don't sashay. I don't frequent that establishment. And I have better things to do than stand here and—"

"Better things to do? That doesn't sound like 'nothing' to me."

"My business is no concern of yours." She turned around to dismiss him.

He fell into step beside her. "Aren't you even a little curious why I was following you?"

"Not particularly." She yanked down the sunglasses.

"Okay." He matched her, step for step, and didn't say another word. He tipped his hat to a few of the townsfolk and waited. Wade hadn't always been this patient. In his younger days he'd been known for his hot blood and his blazing temper. But he'd mellowed during his midtwenties. And he had the advantage here. She wanted to be rid of him, so she would either have to speak to him again or accept his company. He looked forward to either decision.

Her floral scent floating between them, the sunlight shimmering off her blond hair, she stopped on the sidewalk and peered over her sunglasses at him. "What do you want, Wade?"

Her respect? Her trust? Damned if he knew. "It's not what I want but what Andrew wanted."

"Don't play word games with me about my brother." She almost snapped at him, and he realized that the unhealed wound in her heart was responsible for the rawness in her voice. She'd adored her brother, tagging after Andrew into her midteens, shooting hoops with them in the park and getting underfoot. Andrew hadn't minded, and Wade had enjoyed teasing the prickly princess. But they hadn't run into one another that often. Andrew hadn't brought his friends home much, and as Kelly's popularity increased into her late teens, she'd found her own group of friends. Wade and Kelly might not ever have even spoken if not for Andrew—and now he was gone.

"I'm sorry. I miss him, too." Wade ran a hand through his hair. "Let's start over."

"From ten minutes ago? Or eighteen years ago?"

She was referring to the first time they'd met. At ten years old, Wade had been the terror of the schoolyard and a class-A bully, copying his father, his only role model up to that point in his life. Wade had caught a stray ball from a group of kindergarteners playing kick ball. No one dared ask him for the ball—except five-year-old Kelly. She'd skipped over in her immaculate yellow ruffled dress, smiled at him like an angel and had plucked the ball right out of his hands, murmuring a sweet thank-you. He'd been so stunned at her audacity that he'd just stood there and let her get away with it.

Wade didn't answer her rhetorical question. "I spoke to your brother the night he died."

"And?" she prodded.

"He said that if anything happened to him that I should look after you."

Her tone turned all businesslike. "What do you mean—if anything happened to him? Are you saying my brother expected trouble?"

"I'm not sure. He sounded more excited than concerned. I didn't question him thoroughly."

"Why not?" Her voice turned sharp enough to slice and dice, and he refrained from wincing, especially since he'd asked himself that same question a hundred times.

"The saloon was packed. I was shorthanded and I expected him to be over within the hour."

She stood still for a moment, clearly thinking. "Have you mentioned your conversation to Sheriff Wilson?"

He shook his head. "I've spoken to Mitch, Deputy Warwick. He's looking into it for me on the QT."

"Why on the QT?"

He squared his shoulders and it only helped a little to know that she wasn't prying into his personal life but trying to understand the situation with her brother. "Sheriff Wilson isn't exactly a fan of the Lansing family. Deputies don't like answering domestic squabbles." And his folks had habitually fought every Friday and Saturday night. Deputies had stopped at his house as often as the local coffee shop.

He refrained from mentioning that he'd never liked Sheriff Wilson, but Mitch was an all-right deputy. The man had compassion, probably learned the hard way since growing up half Native American wasn't easy in these parts.

To give her credit, Kelly didn't fault Wade—at least out loud. "If you hear anything from Deputy Warwick, you'll let me know?"

"Sure." He wished he could see her eyes that she'd hidden behind those sunglasses.

"You needn't worry about looking after me. I'm fine."

Once again Kelly dismissed him, her booted feet taking the steps, two at a time, up Doc Swenson's front porch. Wade almost left her to her business. But when Doc opened the front door and stepped onto the porch, Wade decided this meeting had nothing to do with a personal medical problem.

At eighty years of age and Mustang Valley's only doctor, Swenson conducted his business inside where he'd converted two downstairs bedrooms into patient consultation rooms, or in the former dining room where he now performed autopsies for the sheriff's department.

The town desperately needed a younger doctor but like most small towns, Mustang Valley didn't have the population to support one of the medical facilities to induce a physician to move here. Doc had delivered most of the townsfolk around these parts, including Kelly and Andrew. When Wade's folks couldn't pay the bill, Doc had treated the thirteen-year-old Wade's broken leg for free. These days, for more serious problems, folks usually made the one-hour drive to Dallas or Fort Worth.

Kelly shook Dr. Swenson's hand. "Hi, Doc. Thanks for agreeing to talk to me. I know you're busy." When Wade stepped up on the porch beside her, she stiffened. "Excuse me, but I don't remember inviting you to join us."

Doc put his hand on Kelly's shoulder. "It's better if Wade's here. Just two hours ago, we had a couple of kids throw a rock through the front window. Probably just a prank." He jerked a thumb at a broken pane temporarily fixed with duct tape. "But I'd feel better if Wade walked you back."

Wade nodded. "Yes, sir." But he thought it odd that Doc believed she needed protection against a couple of juvenile delinquents and wondered if he had an ulterior motive.

Kelly looked up at the porch roof as if seeking heavenly patience, then back at Doc and ignored Wade. "Fine. Doc, I wanted to ask you about Andrew's death."

Doc gestured to a swing on his front porch. "Please, sit. I need to rest these old bones every chance I get—which isn't often enough these days."

Kelly settled on the swing, careful to leave Wade plenty of room so they wouldn't be touching. Normally he might have deliberately crowded her—just to irritate her some more. But he couldn't do that with her looking so distressed about Andrew, and behaved himself, sitting on the opposite end of the swing.

"Doc, the sheriff said my brother died of smoke inhalation."

Doc sat in a rocker and lit his pipe. "I assure you, he didn't suffer any pain."

"You could tell that from the autopsy?" Wade asked.

"Yes."

Kelly twisted her hands in her lap, noticed what she was doing and then grasped one hand firmly in the other. "I don't see how Andrew could have fallen asleep at his desk. When I spoke to him at midnight, he was wide awake and excited and told me he was working on something interesting."

"Did he say what?" Wade asked.

"No." She focused on he doctor. "What else did the autopsy reveal?"

Doc puffed on his pipe and blew out a ring of smoke. "Nasty habit. Don't ever start. Smoking causes cancer, you know."

He took his pipe from his mouth and pursed his lips, eyeing her with a scowl. "I didn't want to mention this at the funeral, and I'm not supposed to tell you this now, but Andrew didn't die from the fire."

"He didn't?"

"He died from a bullet to his head."

"Oh…my…God." Kelly turned white. "Andrew was murdered?"

## Chapter Two

*Murdered?*

Kelly's suspicion had proven correct. Still, having her hunch confirmed proved a shock. Her nerves jerked as if a bomb had gone off and rattled her to the core. At first she feared she might faint, but then, with an inner fortitude, she inhaled a deep breath, squared her sagging shoulders and looked Doc straight in the eyes, listening to his explanation.

"A bullet indicates Andrew's death was an accident, suicide or murder," Doc told them bluntly.

Wade defended his friend. "It wasn't an accident. Andrew didn't keep a gun in the office and he certainly didn't kill himself."

"Why was this kept a secret?" Kelly demanded with unconcealed bitterness. She might have turned white but she hadn't fainted and her brain was working perfectly as the question burst from her.

"Sheriff Wilson wanted me to keep the particulars quiet while he investigated."

"Is this the usual procedure?"

"No, but it's not that *unusual,* either. If the shooter thinks we've attributed Andrew's death to the fire he started, to cover up the shooting, then the sheriff might have a better chance of catching the killer.''

''That may be so.'' Kelly stood, trembling with shock and indignation, wishing she hadn't been so wrapped up in her grief, that she'd followed up on her suspicions sooner. ''But he had no right to keep this from our family. I'd say the sheriff has some explaining to do. Thanks for the information, Doc.''

''Anytime. And be careful. I don't want anything happening to you.''

''I'll be fine.''

''I'll make sure she stays that way.'' Wade shook Doc Swenson's hand and walked down the steps with her. She half expected Wade to try to talk her out of going to the sheriff, but he remained quiet.

''What are you thinking?'' she asked him.

''I was making a mental list of all the people we should talk to.''

''We?''

''I'm not letting you do this alone.''

''I appreciate your wanting to look after me, but...''

He looped his arm through hers. ''It's not necessary?''

''I'm not sure about that.'' She wasn't going to turn down help from any quarter. Wade could be useful. He knew about a side of Andrew that her brother had sheltered her from. He also heard things at the saloon that might be handy. On the other hand, he was big and strong, and she didn't trust herself around Wade. Years ago she'd had a schoolgirl crush on him, but hadn't even considered there could be anything between them since her parents had clearly disapproved of Wade.

She trusted her parents' judgment, so she really didn't like the effect he had on her now. She liked the way he'd looped his arm through hers. She liked his intention to follow through on his promise to her brother. And she liked the concerned look in his eyes. Mix that with his flat-out determination to stick with her, and the man was downright irresistible. Yet never once in all the years she'd known him had he indicated even a smidgen of interest in her beyond as his friend's kid sister.

Considering her interest in him, she should keep her distance. He was all wrong for her. Yet she owed it to her brother to seek justice and, to be fair, she'd have a better chance of success if she accepted Wade's help. Although she'd lived in Mustang Valley all her life, he knew people that she didn't.

As long as he proved helpful, she'd let him stick around. But if he interfered, tried to dissuade her or tried to take over, she'd dump him so fast his head would spin. Satisfied with her plan, she picked up her pace.

Just to keep him from getting too familiar, she removed her arm from his. His touch might be gentlemanly and brotherly, but she didn't relish the way she reacted to him. "Andrew was murdered. If I start poking my nose in where it doesn't belong, the wrong person might notice."

"I'm glad you're going to be reasonable."

She bristled. "I'm always reasonable."

"I'm sure that's true—from your perspective."

"What's that supposed to mean?"

He didn't answer, which infuriated her. Sometimes she had the feeling they came from not just different parts of town but different planets. Maybe that was why he'd always fascinated her. He was so different from the college guys she'd dated.

Wade's voice remained soft but was threaded with steel. "Just so we're agreed. When you go talk to the sheriff, we go together."

She nodded. "Who else is on your mental list?"

"The short list? The fire chief. Andrew's associates at Lambert & Church. Debbie West. And Mitch, the deputy I told you about."

"I vote we start with the sheriff. But I have to meet Cara for lunch." Kelly checked her watch. "Why don't I meet you at the sheriff's station at two?"

"What? You don't want to invite me to do lunch?"

She rolled her eyes skyward. "You wouldn't be interested in our girl talk."

"You'd be surprised what interests me."

She waved him down the street. "Go away, Wade." Knowing from experience that there was no faster way to discourage his company, she added, "Besides lunch, I have some shopping to do."

OVER TUNA SALADS and Dr. Peppers in Dot's sandwich shop, Kelly filled Cara in, recapping her conversation with Doc about her brother's murder and Wade's offer to help figure out what had happened. The high-backed booth gave them some privacy, but Kelly kept her voice down below the croon of a Garth Brooks song over the speaker system, well aware that in small towns like Mustang Valley gossip traveled faster than e-mail.

"So Wade and I are talking to Sheriff Wilson next," Kelly told Cara, pleased with her progress and more determined than ever to keep asking questions.

Cara snapped a bread stick and swirled it in her dressing. "Back up. Slow down. What's with the Wade-and-me stuff?"

"He offered to help. I accepted."

"This is Cara you're talking to, sweetie." Cara crunched down on the bread stick and swallowed. "I happen to know you've had a crush on that guy since practically forever."

"*Had* being the operative word."

"Yeah, right."

The two friends exchanged glances and both chuckled. Kelly saw no point in hiding anything from Cara. Her friend might disapprove, she might speak her mind, but they always backed each other up.

When they were teenagers, Kelly's parents had been a big factor in the boys she'd chosen to date. But perhaps she should reconsider their influence. After all, she was no longer a kid but a college graduate.

"Okay. Wade's still got these very cool gray eyes. I admit it, there's a certain spark there. At least on my side. However, he's still treating me like Andrew's little sister."

"And you don't like it?"

"I like the way his chest and shoulders fill out his tacky T-shirt in all the right places." She held up a hand to stall Cara's protest. "But that doesn't mean I can't accept his help without becoming…involved. I don't judge a man on just his looks."

"Wade's not like those college guys you go with. He's dangerous. I don't like the idea of you and him together. It's like trusting a hungry wolf to guard a newborn calf."

"Andrew trusted him," Kelly countered.

"And look where he is now."

Kelly didn't bother to hide the pain that statement caused. "I can't believe you said that."

"Sorry. My reporter instincts took over. Going in for the kill to win an argument is my specialty." Cara reached over the table, her eyes filled with remorse, and patted Kelly's hand. "But hurting my friend is unacceptable."

Kelly shoved her half-eaten salad away. "Apology accepted. I guess I'm overly sensitive these days."

"Of course you're overly sensitive. Who wouldn't be after losing their brother? You're not yourself and that's one of the reasons I'm worried about you hanging out with Wade. I'll admit he can be useful. He knows almost everyone, and he and Andrew were tight."

"But?"

"But you're especially vulnerable right now. These last weeks have been rough. And you know Wade's reputation is…"

"Just say it."

"He's a hard man to read, and at the same time he's a gifted observer. I've seen him at work behind that bar. He can fix food and serve drinks and act totally absorbed in his work, but now and then it pops out how he's exceptionally aware of his customers. It's almost as if he senses trouble before it starts—like he has sensory antennae, alerting him to what is awry, out of place or simply off.''

''Those aren't bad traits.''

''Yeah, but he keeps his own counsel and runs that saloon like it's his own private kingdom. He's always in charge. I've seen him toss out three-hundred-pound drunks without breaking a sweat or resorting to pulling the knife he keeps strapped to his ankle.''

''He's a skilled marksman, too,'' Kelly added, recalling the picture Andrew had taken of Wade holding a trophy. ''He wins the skeet-shooting competition at the state fair every year. But so what if he doesn't need a bouncer at that saloon of his? Andrew says—said—Wade could be trusted. I figured if there's trouble, he's a good person to have on my side.''

''Yeah, as long as he's not gunning for you.'' Cara drummed her fingers on the table. ''Trouble has a way of finding that man. And the women, old and young, are still attracted to him like mares to a stallion.''

''Give me a little credit. We won't do anything that I don't want.''

Cara shot her a skeptical grin. ''And what exactly do you want from him?''

Kelly paid for their meal with a credit card. ''We can discuss it while you help me pick out a thoroughly intimidating new outfit.''

"You changing outfits for the sheriff or for Wade?" Cara asked.

"Stop grilling me," Kelly half demanded, half complained, knowing her friend meant well but would try to boss her until she put a stop to it. "I know what I'm doing."

"Sure you do." Cara checked her watch. "I don't have much time. Some of us have to work for a living."

Kelly rolled her eyes. "You love that job so much, if the *Mustang Gazette* didn't pay you, you'd work there for free."

"And I've got an interview lined up with Mayor Daniels over his election campaign."

"You're not working on one of your exposés where you've got to go undercover?" Kelly asked.

Cara shook her head. "Not this week, but stay tuned. Anyway, how about I catch up with you later?"

"Okay."

"And Kelly…"

"Yes?"

"Be careful."

"Would you please stop worrying? I'll be fine."

SURELY THAT COULDN'T BE Kelly waiting for him in front of the police station, wearing an outfit Wade classified between summer-break bragging and *Vogue* good-looking? He swallowed hard and reminded himself that his friend's little sister was taboo territory. The fact that Andrew was no longer alive to remind him didn't entitle Wade to forget she was off-limits.

Still, keeping his eyes above her neck was going to be more difficult than controlling a rowdy Saturday night crowd at the Hit 'Em Again Saloon. The contrast between her lace V-neck blouse and string of pearls that dipped between her breasts and her classic smile was almost enough to make Wade spin around and head elsewhere—except he'd promised Andrew to watch out for his little sister.

Wade sighed and kept walking with his teeth gritted in determination. He considered himself fairly knowledgeable about women and their clothes, but Kelly had knocked him off balance for the second time that day.

What in hell did she think she was doing? After working behind a bar he'd learned to recognize that the way a woman dressed said quite a bit about her personality and her mood. Kelly always wore classy, expensive, designer stuff that said hands off. Now her expensive fitted lace blouse stretched across a chest that had suddenly grown ample—no doubt due to some clever underwires designed to tease and entice.

Judging by the heat shooting directly south, he was "enticed" all right. *Down boy.* Kelly was still Kelly. First and foremost she was one high-maintenance lady. Her manicures alone likely cost more than his electric bill.

He had no doubt she was dressing this way for a reason. If she thought the sheriff might be distracted, she would likely be proven correct. No red-blooded male could possibly look at her without his mouth watering. She still wore her hair up, but some of it now tumbled down, curling around her face, one jaunty lock over the corner of her left eye. And those knotted pearls that tucked into the hollow of her breasts taunted his fingers to touch.

She waved at him and the movement caused her breasts to rise, drawing his gaze to her chest. "Nice."

She eyed him with a glint of amusement. "You think I look good in blue?"

"I wasn't talking about your shirt."

"Oh." For a moment her eyes widened as if startled, then she eased into a dangerous smile and looped her arm through his. "Good."

He didn't know what he thought when she didn't act the least insulted by his direct reference to her assets. On the one hand, she seemed more touchable by showing a hint of skin, but contradictorily, he wanted her more than he ever had before. Sure, he'd noticed that Kelly was cute, but he'd never really considered getting together with her. First, there had been Andrew who wouldn't have been pleased, and second, there had always been this unbreachable wall between them. However, the wall had cracks, ones he couldn't seem to stop himself from peeping through.

He frowned at her. "You going to tell me exactly what you're up to before we go inside?"

"Sheriff Wilson already thinks I'm a piece of fluff." She didn't sound resentful, just stated the obvious. "So I went out of my way to reinforce his attitude by buying this shirt."

"Why?"

"Suppose he's hiding more than the fact that my brother was murdered?"

"Like what?"

Wade didn't believe that just because the sheriff wore a badge that he was an upright citizen. But he had no quarrels with the man, either. Wilson's deputies left the saloon alone and Wade took care not to give them reasons to hassle him or his patrons. And he'd like to keep it that way.

"I don't know," she said. Together they entered the Sheriff's Department. "That's why we're here. To ask questions."

"Okay." He wondered if she had a plan or intended to play this by ear. He also wondered if those tight jeans made her hips appear to sway more than usual or if she'd deliberately changed her walk to a sexy swagger.

Kelly headed straight to the front desk, seemingly unaware of the attention several deputies gave her. "We're here to see Sheriff Wilson."

"You have an appointment?" asked a male receptionist who wore a headset and didn't look up from his computer.

"No, sir. But it's real important that I talk to him."

"I'm sure it is." The male officer looked up, then looked again before dismissing her. "He's busy, but if you care to wait…"

Kelly leaned forward and whispered loudly, "You don't understand, sir. This is *personal*. My brother died and I have so many unanswered questions. Sheriff Wilson would much prefer hearing what I have to say in private. However, if you insist, I could go public…"

Wade clamped his teeth together to prevent himself from grinning. Kelly had insinuated that she had crucial information about Andrew and if the desk officer knew what was good for him, he'd give them immediate access to his boss.

The officer pushed a few buttons on a speakerphone, then mumbled into his microphone before jerking his thumb down the hall. "The sheriff will see you now. Third door on your left."

Sheriff Wilson sat in a loose gray uniform behind his desk, a burning cigar in his hand despite the No Smoking sign on the building's front doors. In his fifties, tall and rangy, he had tough, leathery skin that bespoke a hard life-style.

His gaze wandered from Kelly's face to her chest and stayed there until Wade cleared his throat. But that only earned Wade a scowl from Kelly before she turned a high-wattage grin on the sheriff.

"What can I do for you, Kelly?"

"Sheriff, I just wanted to thank you for all your help. It was kind of you to come to my brother's funeral."

"I'm truly sorry for your loss."

Wade wondered where she was going with this conversation. He could tell Sheriff Wilson was just as curious and antsy. No doubt he had more important things on his plate.

Kelly's tone turned weepy. "My brother…he was very special to me. Everyone loved Andrew. I just don't understand why anyone would have wanted to murder him." She opened her purse, removed a tissue and dabbed at her eyes that brimmed with tears.

"Murder?" The sheriff looked from Wade to

Kelly, ignoring his smoking cigar. "Who said anything about murder?"

Wade didn't say a word, but marveled at how she was manipulating the sheriff with her antics. Kelly was just full of surprises. He recalled Kelly had starred in a play during her senior year of high school, but she hadn't displayed this kind of emotional depth back then. Obviously, her acting abilities had improved and Wade wondered if she was playing him, too. But since he'd already agreed to help her, what would be her angle?

Kelly sobbed and her chest quivered. "Wasn't Andrew shot with an 11 mm gun?"

"No, 9 mm." The sheriff's gaze snapped upward from her chest as he realized what he'd just admitted. He raised the cigar to his lips and puffed, probably stalling as he considered his options. "May I ask how you learned—"

Kelly let the tissue trail over her neck. "I want to know who did it."

"The case is under investigation."

"Sheriff, I know you must be doing everything you can, but it's been weeks and weeks. My parents will be devastated to learn that Andrew's death wasn't an accident and that his murderer is still free."

The sheriff didn't exactly squirm in his seat but a bead of sweat broke out on his brow. Kelly's father was a powerful man in Mustang Valley and the sheriff needed his support to keep his job. That he'd kept a secret about Andrew's murder from Mr. McGovern wouldn't sit well with Kelly's father.

The sheriff stubbed out his cigar in an ashtray,

reached across his desk and patted her shoulder. "Look, there's no point in telling your parents what really happened until I find Andrew's killer."

"I don't understand. His family knew him best. Surely we can help, and you haven't even asked us any questions." Kelly's eyes opened wide. "Unless you consider us suspects?"

"Of course not." The sheriff spoke soothingly, patronizingly. Police procedure dictated that everyone would be a suspect until proven otherwise. "Sometimes it's better to keep an investigation quiet. We don't want to scare away the suspect. We want to catch him, right?"

Kelly sniffled. "Yes."

"So let me do my job, okay?"

Wade figured he'd been silent long enough. "Sheriff, I believe Kelly would like you to keep her informed of your investigation."

"Yes, please," Kelly piped in, twisting the screws some more. "That would make me feel ever so much better in keeping a secret from Daddy."

Sheriff Wilson shook his head. "I'm not at liberty to share the facts in this case with you. However, after we catch your brother's killer, Kelly, I assure you that you'll be the first to know."

"Just how long do you expect that to take?"

"I wish I could tell you. I'd like nothing better than to solve this case and put a murderer behind bars, but I won't make you a promise I can't keep. I just don't know how long our investigation will take."

Kelly stuffed the tissue back into her purse, her eyes once again dry. "Thank you, Sheriff. I guess there's no reason to upset Daddy. For now. But promise me...you will place your best deputies on this?''

''Absolutely.''

Wade shook hands with the sheriff and escorted Kelly from the building. ''That was quite a performance.''

As soon as they strode out, she dropped the sexy walk. Her voice turned tart. ''I'd hoped to learn more. A 9 mm is a real popular gun, isn't it?''

''Yeah. And considering this is Texas, that information may not help us much.''

''Maybe I'll learn more at Lambert & Church. I'm heading there next.''

''Uh, Kelly.''

''Yeah?''

''You changing clothes again?''

She winked at him. ''Absolutely.''

# Chapter Three

Kelly didn't know if any of the partners would be in at Lambert & Church, but she assumed one of the associates would have time to talk to her—even if she and Wade arrived without an appointment. She'd changed into the conservative navy suit with gold buttons that she'd picked out that morning and added hose, shoes and a bag to match before pulling her hair back and up into a severe bun. In the rest room at the *Mustang Gazette*, she wiped off most of her makeup and peered at herself in the mirror. She looked like one of those clueless summer law clerks whom Andrew had always liked to tease. In other words, perfectly unremarkable.

With Wade waiting for her to exit, she took a deep breath, hurriedly stashed her jeans and lace top in Cara's office, then headed through the front doors of the busy building. Outside, the humidity had risen along with the temperature into the mideighties. Gray clouds scudded across the sky, threatening a May shower. Azaleas and bluebonnets bloomed in hanging baskets along the sidewalk. And the townsfolk nodded friendly hellos or tipped their hats to passersby.

They strode past Mayor Daniels's campaign headquarters where red, white and blue balloons attached to parking meters outside whipped about in the wind. A banner had come loose and flapped, a broken cord dangling.

"Andrew told me you were a fashion plate, but I thought he exaggerated," Wade teased as he walked beside her wearing the same jeans and dark blue shirt he'd worn since this morning.

"Dressing for the part gives me confidence."

"You look like confidence personified."

"Thank you," she said as self-assurance welled up in her.

Kelly was surprised his patience with her investigation hadn't worn thin by now, but although his long legs ate up a steady pace on the sidewalk, he didn't hurry her. He also didn't pepper her with questions. Unlike the men she'd dated, some of whom could have filled up the Grand Canyon with their compliments, Wade's simple words touched her. That he actually seemed willing to let her take the lead, she appreciated even more.

Wade opened the door for her at Lambert & Church and the cool air-conditioning caused goose bumps to form on her skin. Or perhaps it was the stench of the burned annex out back where Andrew had died. Although a construction company had cleared the burned timbers, the scorched earth still reeked of smoke.

Kelly headed straight for the receptionist. "Hi, Wanda." She greeted the friendly woman who answered the phones and guarded passage to the inner sanctum. "I'd like to speak with Mr. Lambert or Mr. Church, please."

"Sorry, Kelly. Mr. Lambert's in court and Mr. Church has a meeting with Mayor Daniels." Wanda spoke softly. "I want to tell you again how sorry I am about Andrew. We all miss him."

"Thanks."

Beside her Wade squeezed her hand as if he realized how difficult it still was for her to talk about the loss of her brother. But for Andrew's sake, she had to be strong.

"If there's anything I can do—" Wanda's phone rang and she answered it, then transferred the call. "If you like, I can make you an appointment for next week."

Kelly was considering the time slots Wanda offered her just as Lindsey Wellington breezed through the front doors. Kelly recognized the woman lawyer as one of Andrew's co-workers but didn't know her well. A newcomer to Mustang Valley, Lindsey wore her blouse buttoned up to her neck and a long-sleeved jacket as if she still lived in Boston, where Kelly knew she was from.

"Kelly McGovern." Lindsey shifted her documents and stuck out her hand, shaking Kelly's then Wade's as Kelly made introductions.

Lindsey shoved back her shiny brown hair and surveyed them with piercing blue eyes. "I didn't expect you so soon. But please come into my office."

"You're expecting me?" Kelly looked at Wade, who shrugged and appeared puzzled, too.

"Would you like a cup of coffee, tea or a soda?"

Lindsey asked as they followed her into her office
where stacks of legal documents perched on top of
file cabinets and flowed in a river across the floor.
In contrast, her desk was immaculate.

"No, thanks," Kelly answered for both of them.

Lindsey walked behind her desk, opened a closet
door and spoke over her shoulder. "You didn't get
my phone message?"

"I'm afraid not."

"Well, I'm glad you came." Lindsey picked up
a carton and set it down on her desk right in front
of them in a forthright manner. "Before I moved in
here, Andrew had this office. When he relocated to
the annex, he forgot to take some of his things. I
thought you'd want them."

At the familiar smell of Andrew's faded brown
leather jacket, Kelly's throat clogged and her voice
hitched. "Thanks."

"There's not much here." Lindsey's tone, although brusque and polite, still managed to convey
sympathy. "A few family pictures. Some work
notes. Just old memos and junk he forgot to move."

That old junk was all she had left of her brother.
Oh, God. Kelly hadn't known this would be so hard.
Dealing with his death struck her at the oddest and
most unexpected times.

She grappled for self-control. Wade had taken a
chair beside her, seemed to understand her difficulty
and inserted himself smoothly into the conversation.
"Lindsey, did Andrew have any enemies here?"

Lindsey's eyes widened. "At the firm? Everyone
gets along."

"What about clients?" Wade persisted. "Surely

Andrew might have had a few criminals who believed he could have defended them better?''

"Possibly. But they're in jail." Lindsey frowned, her gaze cutting from Wade to Kelly with sharp suspicion. "What's all this about? And why are you here if you didn't get my message?"

Kelly finally collected herself by ignoring that box of Andrew's. "We don't think the fire was an accident." She didn't reveal that the killer had used the fire to cover up a shooting. If the sheriff wanted to keep his investigation quiet, Kelly would abide by the man's wishes.

"You're implying the fire was deliberate?" Lindsey spoke in her strong Boston accent. "We're talking murder?"

"Yes," Kelly admitted. "But please keep this to yourself. The sheriff wants it that way."

"All right. I always liked your brother." Lindsey sounded both sympathetic and careful. Clearly cautious and holding back, she peered at them as if trying to make up her mind about something.

"What?" Kelly's heart hammered her ribs. "If you know anything that might help us figure out who killed my brother…anything at all," Kelly pleaded, "tell us."

"I probably shouldn't—"

"—but you will."

"—give you this." Lindsey opened a file cabinet and used a key to unlock a compartment. "Andrew was working on these papers right before he died. It's a copy of a file." Lindsey spilled the rest. "I think Andrew left this here for safekeeping, but I have no idea why."

"What is it?" Wade asked.

"It's a contract offer to buy the family ranch of Andrew's girlfriend."

Debbie's family was moving? Andrew had never said a word to Kelly about it, but then, he didn't like to talk about his girlfriend since the family had clearly disapproved of her. And due to that lack of communication, Kelly had no idea if this file could be important. Perhaps Wade knew more than she did, and she made a mental note to ask him about Debbie and her family later.

Wade reached for the documents. "Is there anything unusual about the offer?"

"None that I can see." Lindsey frowned at them. "But maybe you should talk to the family."

"We will." Kelly stood. "Everything you've told us is confidential. No one will know where those papers came from. After all, Andrew could have left them at home."

Lindsey motioned her to sit. "There's one more person you might question."

"Who?"

"I shouldn't be telling you this." Lindsey shrugged, then sighed. "But I'd like to see justice done."

"I don't want to compromise your position, but any help you can give us would be appreciated."

Lindsey gestured with her hands. "It's nothing that wasn't reported in the *Mustang Gazette* just a few months ago."

"I was away at college then," Kelly told her.

"Andrew represented Sean McCardel during his divorce last year. Apparently the client wasn't satisfied with his representation. When the judge awarded full custody of the kids to his wife, he blamed Andrew. Apparently the man blew up on the courthouse steps, vowing to get even. Of course, it may have just been talk.''

Kelly would ask Cara. If her friend hadn't covered the story, she would know who had. Kelly stood, walked around the desk and hugged Lindsey. ''Thanks so much for all your help.''

WADE DIDN'T WANT to be impressed with the way Kelly had handled Lindsey, but he was. As he carried Andrew's box to her pretty new silver Jaguar and stowed it in the trunk, he realized that Kelly had displayed the exact right mix of sympathy and determination to elicit Lindsey's help. Kelly might look and act like a fashion plate, but she had keen instincts about people. While he wouldn't call her tactics outright manipulation, he would call them brilliant. The way she won people to her cause, Mayor Daniels would have been smart to have hired her on his campaign staff.

Already today she'd learned from the doctor that Andrew hadn't died in an accidental fire but from a bullet. The sheriff had admitted to her that the gun was a 9 mm, and now Lindsey had just given her several new leads. And they hadn't yet had time to go through Andrew's box.

Kelly glanced up at the darkening thunderclouds. ''I want to change back into jeans before we head out to Debbie's ranch. Could we please take your truck?''

''Good idea.'' Not only would Debbie's family

resent her pulling up to their struggling ranch in her nifty new sports car, but with the storm brewing and the roads slick, he'd rather have four-wheel drive. "I'm parked behind the saloon."

Ten minutes later the storm broke, drenching his truck, but they were ensconced safe and dry inside. He switched on his lights and wipers, almost turned up the country station but decided he'd rather talk to Kelly instead—which rocked him back in his seat. Wade had always liked women. He liked their scents, their smiles, the way they moved. And he especially enjoyed how Kelly sugarcoated her determination with an ultra femininity that conveyed a strength he'd never suspected.

He found her too damn attractive and wondered if she was playing him just as she'd done with the doc, the sheriff and Lindsey. He didn't like that idea at all, but he also didn't understand why it bothered him as much as it did. What was it about her that called to him? Perhaps she was simply his last living tie to Andrew, his best friend since high school.

Wade turned onto the highway. The heavy downpour had caused several cars to pull under the overpass to wait out the storm. With the large-size tires on his truck, he had good traction and the large cab gave him decent visibility, so he proceeded with caution.

"Tell me about Debbie," Kelly requested, her eyes focused before them on the road, her tone firm—and yet he sensed a hesitancy to pry into Andrew's private life.

He risked a glance at her. Her eyes looked troubled. "What do you want to know?"

She rested her hands loosely in her lap. The air-conditioning cleared the moisture from the windshield and carried her scent to him, making the cab seem intimate and cozy, especially with the rain pattering the roof.

"Andrew was going to bring her home to Sunday breakfast. He didn't care what our folks thought. He was certain of his choice and determined to marry her. But did he love her? Or was he rebelling against my father?"

Astute questions and ones Wade wasn't sure he knew the answers to. "He didn't talk much about her to me."

"But you saw them together?"

"He brought her to the saloon most Saturday nights."

"And?"

"And what?" Distinct discomfort about answering her questions made him stall.

"What was your impression of her?"

He reminded himself that betraying Andrew wasn't possible. The most he could do for his dead friend was help his sister seek justice. "If you're asking me if Debbie was with Andrew because he was successful and had a bright future or because she loved him, I wouldn't know."

"You're holding out on me," Kelly complained. "I'm not asking you for facts—just your impression. Certainly you must have given some thought to Andrew's choice in a wife?"

"Frankly, I thought he could do better." Wade swerved around fallen debris on the highway. "But you know Andrew—"

"He wanted to fix the world."

"Exactly. He liked to be needed and therefore he tended to pick women in distress."

"What did Debbie need from him besides legal help with her property?"

Kelly obviously didn't know much at all, and Wade found himself reluctant to reveal his friend's secrets. First, he didn't want to cause the McGovern family more pain. Second, he had to remind himself once again that Andrew was dead and talking to his sister wasn't a betrayal. Still he knew his revelation would come as a shock and braced himself before speaking sympathetically. "Debbie had been married and divorced."

"You're sure?" Kelly's brows lifted in surprise and consternation.

"Yeah."

"How could I not know that? How could my *parents* not know that? Mustang Valley is simply too small for gossip not to have reached us. Daddy has all kinds of connections and not even Cara knew Debbie was married, because she would have told me."

"According to Andrew, Debbie married Niles Deagen after she got pregnant her sophomore year in high school."

Kelly gulped. "She has a child?"

"She had a miscarriage. So the hush-hush elopement and Vegas wedding were unnecessary after all. She wanted the marriage annulled, but Niles wouldn't agree to it, although he did keep it quiet to avoid looking like a fool."

Trouble seemed to follow Debbie like a dark

shadow. While Wade had nothing against her personally, he always had felt she came attached to too many problems. Which was exactly why Andrew no doubt had found her irresistible. His friend had a thing for the underdog, while Wade preferred to keep things simple.

So what was he doing with Kelly? Because sure as hell, there was nothing simple about her. She came with her own set of problems that slowly but surely were becoming his. But even if he could withhold his help, he could never deny Andrew the justice he deserved.

"Why would he look foolish for marrying Debbie?" Kelly asked with an innocence that made him realize once again how protected she'd been. Her folks had made sure she'd only seen the better side of life. Wade didn't blame them. Kelly had a special spark around her that caused optimism in others. She saw the up side in people, expected the best and was rarely disappointed.

"Debbie was sixteen. Her husband was thirty-eight."

"Oh."

"Andrew finally helped her obtain a messy divorce. I heard that Niles still wants her, but that's rumor—not fact."

Kelly didn't let the nasty facts deter her from plunging right in to find out more. "Niles Deagen. Why does that name sound so familiar?"

"He's a big-time Dallas oil man, with a penchant for teenage girls."

"But Debbie's no longer a kid."

"She still looks like a kid. She's flat-chested and

slender-hipped and has that round baby face that makes her appear about twelve.''

Wade didn't understand the man. Wade liked his women full-grown and grown-up. While Kelly would fit his physical requirements, he usually dated women who wanted nothing more from him than a good time. Instinctively he knew that when Kelly hooked up with a man, she would be thinking about the possibility of happily ever after.

Kelly shot him a sharp glance. ''You think Niles could have had anything to do with Andrew's murder?''

''That would be pure speculation.'' But the thought had occurred to Wade. More than once. However, he didn't have a shred of evidence to back up that hunch.

''If he's an oil man, he has the means and a motive.'' Kelly sighed. ''I never thought finding Andrew's killer would be simple, but the more I learn, the more complicated this seems. I keep adding suspects to my list and haven't eliminated anyone.''

He didn't like the idea of Kelly getting discouraged. Not when she'd done such a good job of keeping herself together.

''Hey, chin up. Today's only the first day. You're doing great.''

''Maybe I should ask Daddy to hire a private investigator.''

''You could.''

''But?''

''He'd be a stranger to Mustang Valley, and the folks here don't open up to outsiders.'' And then

Wade wouldn't have an excuse to spend more time with her.

"I imagine you hear all kinds of gossip in your saloon." She hit him with one of those innocent-sounding, sideways comments that made it difficult to anticipate where she was taking the conversation.

"We've been busy lately. That means I have to draft lots of beer and rustle up my Texas-famous chili. You stop by sometime and I'll serve you up a bowl—on the house."

"Thanks." As if uncomfortable with the notion of them spending time together for any reason other than Andrew, she changed the subject. "So what hot buttons have stirred up the town lately? Does Tony Barker have a shot at defeating Mayor Daniels?"

"I doubt it."

"That's what Cara said, too. Tony was a friend of Andrew's, I should probably stop by and see him."

"Even Andrew, as much as he liked the underdog, didn't think Tony had a chance of defeating the mayor. Daniels's contributors have deep pockets, and the town isn't much interested in local politics these days. Folks are more concerned about the price of beef, land, oil and—"

"What's wrong?"

"Maybe nothing."

She caught him scanning his rearview mirror, glanced over her shoulder, spied the tow truck with its flashing yellow lights. "It's Aaron's Towing. Probably someone broke down in the rain."

Wade checked his speedometer. Fifty-five. The tow truck must be barreling down the highway at eighty mph to be closing the distance between them so fast. It wasn't as if the truck was an emergency vehicle with lives at stake, so to be driving at that speed in the stormy weather wasn't just reckless, but brainless.

Wade pulled over, steering his tires onto the shoulder to give the big truck ample room to pass.

"Wade! He's not passing." Kelly tightened her seat belt and braced her feet on the dash. "He's going to hit us."

Wade overrode his first instinct to hit the brakes. A collision at a slower speed would cause a more forceful impact. Instead he jammed his foot on the gas and took satisfaction as his truck lunged forward.

Kelly tugged on his arm. "Are you crazy?"

"I'm not racing him. I'm trying to avoid a crash." In his mirror he glimpsed the tow truck gaining on him and shook her hand off his arm. "Let me drive."

"He's catching us. I thought this truck was fast."

"It is. But he had a head start." Wade checked the mirror. The tow truck couldn't be more than a few car lengths behind. "Hold on."

"Like I have something else to do?" she muttered.

Wade prayed his truck could pick up enough speed to avoid a crash. But he hadn't recognized the threat soon enough. His late reaction might get them both killed.

"Do something else," Kelly insisted.

He yanked the wheel. Tires screeched and burned rubber. He steered the truck off the road and thanked God for the flat and rolling land of Texas. They smacked through the guardrail and suddenly the truck was airborne. Kelly let out a gasp. He braced for impact, praying the truck wouldn't roll. Praying the tow truck wouldn't come down on top of them. Praying Kelly and he would survive.

Before death, one's entire life was supposed to flash before him. But all Wade could think about was failing in his promise to Andrew—that he'd failed to take care of Kelly McGovern.

The truck bounced hard. Rolled. Crunched. A vortex of metal spun them and then spit him out.

WADE DIDN'T REMEMBER the truck stopping. Why was he out of the truck when he'd been wearing his seat belt? He'd come to, flat on his back with the rain pelting his face. He had no idea how long he'd been unconscious, but he was soaked to the skin and shivering. The thunderstorm still raged full force, and the sky had darkened with the sun setting behind the clouds.

For a moment he was tempted to just lie there. But then the accident came rushing back. Kelly. He had to find her. She might need him.

He tasted blood, sat up and spit. Despite his seat belt, he'd been thrown out of the truck. Every muscle in his body roared in pain, but he forced himself to his feet, staggered to his truck.

His truck lay upside down, the cab crushed inward, the windshield a spiderweb of cracks on one side, the passenger's window long gone. Bending and dreading what he would find, Wade peered inside. Between the rain and the fading light, he wondered if he could be hallucinating.

The truck was empty.

Just to make sure, he crawled inside, praying her body wasn't wedged against the floorboards. His hand caught on the seat belt strap and tugged free. The end had clearly been slashed with a sharp object, probably leaving just a few frail threads intact, which had torn during the crash.

The chance of one seat belt failing had to be astronomically high. The chance of both of them failing at the same time meant that someone had wanted them dead.

A prickle of ice stabbed down his spine. Wade crawled deeper inside the cab. He felt around, ignoring the bits of glass that sliced his flesh.

Nada.

He wriggled back out, confused and breathing hard.

*Think.*

His cell phone had been crushed. Calling for help wasn't an option.

The tow truck was nowhere to be seen. The highway stretched empty ahead and behind as far as he could see.

Perhaps Kelly had been thrown out of the vehicle like he'd been. She could be lying by the road hurt…or worse. Wade pried open his toolbox and retrieved his flashlight.

After a thorough search, he slumped next to his truck in despair.

No one had passed by in all that time, and he hadn't found any sign of Kelly at all. She was gone.

## *Chapter Four*

Dazed and wet, Kelly shivered in the front seat of a passenger car. She couldn't recall climbing inside the vehicle, couldn't recall the driver's name, couldn't remember anything that had happened since leaving Lambert & Church over an hour ago.

Her head ached, and every time she turned it, a sharp pain sliced down her neck. Her palms stung from road rash and each whipped muscle in her body smarted when she breathed.

The friendly woman driver said she'd found Kelly stumbling down the highway, but Kelly didn't remember that, either. With her scraped palms and wet clothes, she must have been in an accident. Thank God she didn't have total amnesia. She knew who she was and recalled her entire life, everything except the last hour—no doubt due to the golf ball-size knot near her temple.

Kelly looked at her clothes for clues. She wasn't dressed for riding her horse. Jasper hadn't thrown her and left her for greener grass. As Kelly tried to recall what had happened, the pain in her head sharpened, but she forced herself back to her last coherent memory.

She and Wade had been about to…Wade. Something must have happened to him. And suddenly it all came back, the tow truck, Wade's truck rolling, her smacking her head and awakening in the rain. Wade was probably back at the accident site.

"Please, turn around," Kelly requested.

"I need to get you to a doctor," the Good Samaritan driver insisted with gentle firmness. In the dim light of the car's interior, the woman's white hair fluffed around her face in an attractive manner.

"You don't understand." The driver's name came back to her in a flash. "Peggy, I was in an accident. And I wasn't alone. We have to go back."

Peggy plucked a cell phone from her purse. "We'll call 911 and they'll send police and an ambulance."

"But we're closer." Kelly fought down rising panic. "Suppose he bleeds to death. I can't just drive off with you and leave him lying there. Please, turn around."

"Okay, but I didn't *see* any accident." Peggy called 911 and reported the situation, then spoke calmly to Kelly. "When I found you, you were all alone."

Kelly's panic subsided a little as Peggy pulled a U-turn. "Wade swerved off the road to avoid the tow truck." And now, in the dark, they could ride right by and not see him or the truck. "Can you find the spot where you picked me up?"

"I doubt it. This road looks the same for miles

and miles. But we can try, dear. Tell me about your fellah. Is he a good man?''

''He's not mine. He's a friend of my brother's, and yes, he's a good man.'' Funny how she'd answered without hesitation. Wade might have a dangerous reputation, he might have lived a rough life, but he could be counted on, and she instinctively trusted him. ''He was trying to help me....''

*Oh, God.* If anything had happened to him because he had been helping her, she might never forgive herself. She shouldn't have gotten him involved. Her hands shook and she twisted them in her lap, peering through the dark windshield, praying she might spy his truck. A taillight. Something.

She tried to tell herself she would have had the same nauseous worry in her gut over the welfare of anyone who'd been riding with her, but Kelly wasn't accustomed to lying to herself. She liked Wade. Really liked him.

Perhaps someone else had picked up Wade and even now he was back in Mustang Valley, taking a hot shower. No. Wade wasn't the kind of man to leave her behind. If he'd been able, if he'd been conscious, he would have found her. He wouldn't have left her.

If only she had remembered what had happened sooner.

*Please let him be all right,* she prayed.

The driver began to slow. ''I think I found you around here.''

In the dark, this part of the highway looked exactly the same as the rest to Kelly. ''Can you please pull onto the shoulder and turn on your high beams?''

"It would help if we knew which side of the road you crashed on," Peggy suggested, but did as Kelly asked.

*Oh, no.* Kelly almost smacked her forehead, but memory of her head injury stopped her hand in mid-motion. "I'm not thinking clearly. We were on the other side of the road, heading *out* of town."

"You're sure?"

"Yes."

"All right. Let's stay on this side for two miles," Peggy recommended. "I'll keep track on the odometer and then I'll turn around and head back again. But if we don't see anything, I'm taking you into town. Deal?"

Kelly knew Peggy meant well, but she wasn't leaving. Not until she found Wade. She peered up ahead and across the highway and saw movement. Then a light flashed on and off, then back on again. A headlight? A reflector?

"Look!" Kelly pointed.

Peggy angled the car and slowed even more. "That's a man with a flashlight waving us down."

"It's Wade." They were too far away to make out his features, but she knew it had to be him. And the fact that he was well enough to stand by the road and signal made her heart thump wildly against her ribs. He was alive.

The future suddenly seemed brighter. As relief and delight raced through her, she realized that she didn't want to waste more time playing silly games. She wanted to get to know Wade better, and she didn't mind in the least making her feelings clear to him. But she also feared that her growing attraction to Wade might be her way of hanging on to memories of her brother. Andrew had been such a great guy and she'd hated losing him. She didn't understand how anyone would have wanted to kill him. But Andrew, of all people, would have wanted her to be honest with his best friend.

Whatever happened between her and Wade—she wasn't going to hide. Not from herself. Not from him. Life was too precious to squander their days. Or their nights.

A moment later Peggy pulled another turn and stopped. Kelly slid out of the passenger seat and ran toward him, her adrenaline rushing, her mouth dry, her pulse pounding. "Are you all right?"

"I'm fine—now that you're here." Wade's arms closed around her. His shirt was soaked and bloody, but he didn't hesitate to draw her to him. His skin was icy cold, and she snuggled against him, trying to give him some of the warmth she'd gained from the car's heater.

Her parents must have been wrong about Wade, since being within the circle of his arms seemed so right. And perhaps it was time to make her own decisions. She would no longer live solely for her parents' approval. She was a grown woman and could make her own choices. Kelly wanted to tell Wade about her epiphany about him, how she'd realized she'd been suppressing her feelings for no good reason other than a schoolgirl habit, but with Peggy there to overhear every word, she couldn't say what she wanted to.

Wade hugged her for what seemed like much too short a time before stepping back. "I've been searching for you since I woke up."

"After I hit my head, I was dazed. Peggy picked me up as I walked along the highway. It took a while until my memory of the accident came back."

"And then she insisted we turn around and find you," Peggy told him. "I've phoned 911 and the deputies and emergency medical should be here soon. Why don't we all wait in my car where it's warm?"

It seemed like forever until the police wrapped up their investigation. Kelly sat in the back of Peggy's car, snuggling against Wade's side. He tried to move away, but after she claimed she was chilled, wrapped his arm over her shoulder and allowed her to snuggle against him.

After Wade told her about the slashed seat belts, she should have been alarmed. When the deputy informed them that the tow truck had been reported stolen just hours ago, she should have felt doubly unsafe, but she didn't. With Wade's comforting arms around her, she relaxed amid an overpowering belief that they would be all right, that they would find Andrew's killer.

After the paramedics checked her and Wade and they both refused further medical care, they learned that another deputy had found the tow truck several miles up the highway.

And there was no sign of the driver.

DEPUTY MITCH WARWICK gave Wade and Kelly a lift back to Mustang Valley. Kelly had thanked

Peggy for all of her help. A tow truck would haul Wade's totalled vehicle back in the morning. However, Wade's primary concern was not his truck but Kelly's safety.

Maybe he was overreacting, but Wade preferred for Kelly to stay with him rather than go home to her parents' house tonight. Before he broached that controversial topic, he wanted backup, and Mitch seemed just the level-headed guy to agree with him.

In the back seat of the deputy's car, Wade spoke to Kelly, but loudly enough for Mitch to hear, too. "Our questions about Andrew's death today rattled someone badly enough to attempt murder."

"Mustang Valley doesn't have enough law enforcement to protect anyone 24/7. Have you considered leaving town?" Mitch asked from the driver's seat.

The early-evening storm had come and gone, leaving behind a chilly drizzle and even more questions than Wade had that morning. And more suspects. He'd thought he'd known Andrew fairly well, but if he hadn't known Andrew had been murdered, he would never have believed his friend could have stirred up this kind of animosity against him.

"I do have a business to run," Wade answered. Although he had a manager to take care of the saloon when he wasn't there, his personal touch was required to keep things running smoothly.

"I live here," Kelly added. "I can't just turn tail and run. I owe it to my brother to find out what happened."

Mitch took the highway's exit to Mustang Valley.

"Your brother wouldn't have wanted you in danger."

So the level-headed Mitch believed Kelly might still be in danger, too. That confirmation was all Wade required to speak his mind. "Kelly, I'd feel better if you spent the night with me."

"I'm sure you would."

Wade couldn't see her face but heard the amusement in her tone and chuckled. "I'm serious."

"So am I."

"You'd be safer with me. And you don't want to endanger your folks, do you?"

"I could stay with Cara." Kelly didn't sound sure, as if she hadn't considered her plans until now and had yet to make up her mind.

"You really believe two women alone would be less of a target?"

"What kind of target would I be at your place?" Kelly asked, her tone cool.

At her smart comment, Mitch choked back a laugh and Wade had to restrain one as well. However, if the situation wasn't so serious, he would have enjoyed teasing her right back.

Instead, he kept his voice thoughtful. "This isn't about you and me."

"Now I think I'm insulted," she muttered.

This time Wade definitely heard a chuckle from the front seat. How unbelievable that she could feel snubbed when he wouldn't make a move toward her. What nonsense. Out of respect for Andrew, he would keep his hands off her. In fact, if she hadn't claimed to be cold, he wouldn't have allowed her to nestle up against him like a sunbathing cat. "Would you care to elaborate?"

"If you can't admit the basic chemistry between us, you aren't ready for the advanced class."

"You go, girl." Mitch egged her on.

"Enough comments from the peanut gallery," Wade snapped at the deputy before turning back to Kelly. "In case you've forgotten, someone murdered your brother. Probably that same someone tried to kill us this afternoon."

"And we survived. While I understand the need to be careful, I refuse to let my life be dictated by a killer." Wade opened his mouth to interrupt but she kept talking. "Daddy bought me the cutest little Saturday night special for my birthday and I keep it in the glove compartment of my Jag."

"Do you know how to use the gun?" Wade asked, wondering if Andrew had been aware that his little sister carried a gun.

"It's loaded. Daddy said all I needed to know was how to point it and pull the trigger."

"You've never fired the gun?" Wade asked, keeping his voice mild while his anger spiked at her father's irresponsibility. Without practice, the first time she fired the gun, she was as likely to shoot herself as her intended target.

"I've never needed to even take it out of the special pink leather case." She drew herself up proud and straight. "I don't exactly hang out with the kind of people who need shooting."

"And I do?"

She patted his shoulder. "Now I've gone and ruffled your male feathers. I didn't say anything about who you hang with. How could I, when I don't even *know* your friends. Ever since we met up at Doc's this morning, I've known I felt safer with you than going on alone.'' Aggravation edged her tone. ''That's why I accepted your help in the first place. So I think, yes, I'll spend the night with you, Wade. Now make me a happy woman and tell me I can have the bed.''

Hmm. Talk about smooth. She was accepting his invitation and setting rules at the same time. ''What about that great chemistry you said we shared?''

''That's all we're going to share—for tonight, anyway. I'm not in the mood for romance. I have an ugly knot on the side of my head and God knows how many bruises. My blouse is ripped and my shoes scuffed so badly I don't know if I can ever wear them again. Right now a hot bath, clean sheets and a good night's sleep sound like heaven.''

''I can do better than a hot bath.''

''Really?''

''My back deck has a hot tub. If you're not going to let my fingers soothe away your aches and pains, the jets should do the trick.''

She winked at him. ''I didn't bring a swimsuit. But then, I don't suppose that matters, does it?''

DESPITE ASSORTED CUTS and bruises the thought of a nude Kelly in Wade's hot tub caused an immediate and disturbing tingle, then blood surged south. He unlocked the front door of the ranch house that his uncle had left him along with the saloon, hoping her interest in his home would distract her from his too-tight jeans.

He flicked on a light, then adjusted the dimmer to low. "Home, sweet home."

She spun around, taking in the wooden-planked walls, the old two-man hand saw hanging above the sofa, the tan furniture and the shelves of books that lined the wall opposite the stone fireplace. She inspected the only picture he had of his parents, another of him and Andrew and grinned at the blooming white orchid in his kitchen window.

"I'd never have suspected that you liked flowers."

He raised an eyebrow. "There's probably lots you don't know about me."

No doubt she didn't even suspect that he'd read every book on his shelves, either. But then again, he'd seen her father's vast library in his home office and had thought the same thing of Mr. McGovern. But while her father's collection of thick leather volumes looked shiny and new, the pages uncreased— at least, the few he'd thumbed through—Wade's books were worn and frayed, comfortable and familiar friends to get him through some hard nights.

"What would you like first? Food? Coffee? A hot bath?"

"Do you have any juice?" Her eyes sparkled and she headed through the living room and straight to the double glass sliding doors, curiosity in her expression. "This where you keep the hot tub?"

"Yeah." He turned on the DVD, wishing Reba's rich croon would calm his traitorous body, then poured two glasses of juice. Pretending that Andrew was here wasn't working. Neither was pretending that she was simply a woman he'd brought home from the saloon. Because there was nothing simple about Kelly McGovern. Another woman might be moaning and groaning over her bruises. Another woman might run home to daddy. Another woman wouldn't make herself so damn at home that he felt as if he was the intruder. ''Give me a minute to get robes and towels.''

Retrieving the items only took seconds, but he took a moment to lean back against a wall in his darkened hallway, close his eyes and calm his pounding pulse. He drew in a deep breath, and Kelly's tantalizing scent, both feminine and earthy, wafted in through the open doors on a breeze. Reminding himself that she wasn't there for romantic purposes did nothing to cool his ardor.

He wished he could attribute his reaction to the near-death experience. But the truth was that he'd liked her a long time. Although he'd never expected to entertain her in his home, his body seemed to be acting on an accumulation of moments they'd spent together over the years. Moments he hadn't given much significance to until now.

He heard a splash and envisioned her trailing her perfectly manicured nails through the heated water, dipping in a delectable toe and ankle before lowering herself inch by delectable inch into the water. Most likely he had no trouble envisioning her, since he'd seen her swimming at Half-Moon Lake. Was that a sigh of contentment he heard over Reba's melody?

But sharing lake water and his hot tub were two different things. Having her in his home guaranteed he wouldn't sleep tonight. But he'd had no choice.

At least here he could offer her some measure of

protection. The house had a decent alarm system, and if anyone showed, they'd have to go through him to get to her. He wouldn't have allowed her to go outside alone, except the backyard was fenced. Besides, whoever had been after them this afternoon probably didn't yet know their plan had failed. While he fully expected another attempt on their lives, he figured their enemy wouldn't regroup this soon.

Still, he intended to be prepared. His skilled fists and the knife he kept strapped to his ankle might not be good enough protection. Carrying the towels and robes over one arm, two·juice glasses in his hands and a shotgun under his other arm, he headed out onto his deck.

It was black outside with low, threatening thunderclouds blocking any sight of the moon. But the deck lights that absorbed solar energy during the day and emitted soft blue lighting after dark allowed him to see her. Just as he'd suspected, she was already soaking in the tub, her head tilted back, her chin pointed upward, her eyes closed. Every inch the pampered princess, she spoiled the image by shoving a lock of hair from her eyes and revealing a dark smudge that at first he thought was a shadow, but upon inspection proved to be a bruise. She'd be lucky if she didn't have a gigantic shiner under her eye tomorrow.

What was he thinking? She was banged up and hurting and here he was standing salivating over her when she required medical attention. Alcohol to clean her cuts. At the very least, some painkillers.

"I'll be right back." He set the robe and towels

nearby, braced the shotgun within easy reach of the tub and headed inside. Opening his freezer, he grabbed a handful of ice which he wrapped inside a clean hand towel.

What else? Aspirin.

When he returned to the patio, she hadn't moved one inch. But her lips parted into a grin. "This is heaven."

No, heaven would be taking her into his arms, tasting her lips, massaging her shoulders. He'd been about to climb into the tub and join her but found himself hesitating.

While he couldn't see her body, just knowing about her lack of clothing had heat flushing his neck. He didn't want her to know how he was reacting to her, but hiding his arousal didn't seem possible without his body cooperating.

And for some reason that part of his anatomy had developed a sudden rebellious streak. *Down boy*.

He stalled for time and sipped some apple juice. He rarely drank alcohol. With his family's drinking history, he preferred not to test his susceptibility to addiction, so he was perfectly happy with the juice and handed her a glass of her own.

"Thanks," she murmured, her tone throaty and low.

When their fingers touched just briefly, the heat from her flesh darted up his arm and then swooped straight to his lower regions. Gritting his teeth, he backed away, determining that surely distance would allow him to regain a measure of control.

She peered over her juice glass. "Aren't you joining me?"

"One of us has to stand guard."

She sipped her juice and rested the glass on the edge of the redwood tub. Her hold on the glass might be delicate but her tone was anything but. "Let me get this straight. You're standing guard because you think I'm going to attack you?"

He chuckled. "That thought never crossed my mind."

But at her erotic suggestion, his thoughts frothed enthusiastically. What he wouldn't give to have her attack him. He imagined wet, slick flesh pressing him down, her mouth, hot and seeking, taking exactly what she wanted.

She frowned at him. "You're standing guard because you want to impress me with your... equipment?"

Her husky voice and her sweet scent had made him forget that she possessed a truly sharp mind and that the double entendre had no doubt been deliberate. Of course, his forgetfulness might also have something to do with knowing that she sat fewer than two feet from him—without a stitch of clothing on. Or it might be that he knew she wouldn't object to him climbing right into the tub with her, sitting so close their breaths would mingle, their thighs would touch.

No, he couldn't risk it.

Beads of sweat broke out on his forehead and he took another sip of juice. "In case you've forgotten, someone wants to kill us. We can't let down our guard."

"Oh, really?" Her voice tied him in knots with her skepticism. "You thought it was safe enough to let me come out here without you, and now you're trying to tell me that you need to stand guard, like my ancestor Shotgun Sally's lover, Zachary Gale, once did when he protected her from Indians? I don't think so.''

"What's with your family's obsession with that particular ancestor?''

"What do you mean?''

"Andrew told me he wanted to fall in love with the same passion that Zachary loved his Sally.''

"Some families can trace their ancestors back to kings and queens. Some claim fame by tracing their genealogy back to the Mayflower. In my family we're proud to be descendants of Shotgun Sally.''

"But she wasn't nobility. Legends say she was a rebel. You really think you're one of her descendants?''

"Yes. And stop changing the subject.''

She'd caught him. "Huh?''

"Don't 'huh' me. You know I find that particular ancestor fascinating, so you deliberately tried to distract me from your lack of courage.''

He choked on the juice and set it down. "Excuse me?''

"I'm finding your illogical statements absolutely fascinating. Admit it. You don't want to climb into this tub with me.''

He shrugged. "Okay. I don't want to climb into the tub with you.''

"Ah,'' she sipped her juice, her delicate neck tempting his fingers to stroke. "What about if I promise not to bite?''

He didn't answer with words but gave in to temptation and placed his hands on her shoulders. The pulse at her neck leaped, but she held perfectly still as if a movement might break the mood. Standing behind her, he allowed himself the pleasure of kneading away the knots and the tense muscles, soothing sore tendons. Her skin beckoned him to touch, to smooth, to soothe.

"Mmm," she sighed. "You feel so good, I'll give you an hour to stop that."

"And when the hour's up, you'll be putty in my hands?" he teased.

"Something like that." She swirled the liquid in her glass. "So what's the real reason you won't get in this tub with me?"

No way was he answering her question. He removed his hands from her shoulders, stopping the massage. His fingers tingled with sorrow at the sudden lack of her warmth, but he forced them to reach for the washcloth filled with ice instead.

"Where's that knot on your head?"

She touched the tender spot and winced. "Here."

"This should keep down the swelling." Gently he placed the icy cloth on the lump.

"It's cold."

"Ice usually is," he agreed.

"I liked the massage better."

"I'm sure you did. After a while we need to move this to the bruise by your eye."

"But—"

"Think how bad you're going to feel when you look in the mirror at your big black eye or if this lump swells to the size of a grapefruit."

''Not funny. We could have died today, and I decided that since we lived, we should really live.'' She smiled and sipped her juice. ''Maybe you should kiss me where I hurt and make me all better?''

# *Chapter Five*

Kelly stretched and then winced at several sore muscles. But as she awakened in Wade's guest room where she'd slept alone, and recalled last night, she frowned over her behavior. What had happened to the conservative college graduate who was supposed to be spending the summer deciding between a career in law or real estate? Andrew's murder had not only devastated her but taken her to another place.

She couldn't blame a nonalcoholic beverage for her behavior toward Wade, but she must not have been herself or she never would have been so forward. She'd played reluctant to spend the night at his home while riding in the back of the squad car, but Wade hadn't pursued her flirtation as she'd hoped. So she'd changed tactics, and never had she acted so boldly in her life. She wished her excuse was that it wasn't every day she came so close to dying. However, instead of her entire life passing in front of her eyes, she'd seemed able to momentarily set aside everything but her building feelings for Wade. She'd heard of men and women who tossed away their value of abstinence before a partner went off to war. But she didn't even have that excuse. She'd made all those inviting remarks to Wade *after* she'd known she was safe.

On top of the danger, the hot tub had relaxed her to a state where she'd cut loose her inhibitions like a thirty-pound anchor and sailed onward steered by nothing but pure feminine instinct. Okay, she wasn't surprised that she had those impulses. The real shocker was that she'd acted on them while right in the middle of trying to find out who had killed her brother. She felt guilty as hell for reaching out to Wade when Andrew was dead. And yet her brother would have understood her need to connect with a man she liked and respected at a time when she was emotionally shaky. If Andrew had still been alive he would have told her there was nothing wrong with giving and receiving comfort. And while she'd once wondered if her attraction to Wade might have been a longing to hang on to memories of Andrew, she now knew better. She liked Wade, liked the way he treated her.

Her feelings toward Wade seemed to have done a complete 180 in a very short time. Until Andrew's death, Wade had always irritated her, but perhaps she just hadn't recognized the simmering attraction between them until now, when they were sharing so much time together. So her boldness hadn't come out of nowhere but was an accumulated buildup that had reached the do-something-about-it stage, allowing her to make the first move. Although she wasn't sure herself how far she'd intended to go, her invitation had been unmistakable.

And then, after she'd gone and overcome inclinations she'd suppressed for a lifetime, Wade hadn't even joined her in the tub.

He'd acted the perfect gentleman. Damn him. She not only felt like a fool, she had no idea how she would face him this morning. Pretend none of it had happened? She could go with that option. Pretend his rejection didn't matter? But that would be a mockery of her own feelings, and she wouldn't do it.

However unaccustomed she was to being the aggressor, however much she'd been taught to play the flirtatious Southern belle and to practice come-hither looks, she'd enjoyed the part of pursuer and wasn't so sure she wanted to give up the role. Failure didn't sit well with her at any time, never mind with something as important as getting to know Wade better. The fact that he was so valiantly resisting only increased her determination.

She needed a game plan. Obviously some new clothes. She couldn't decide which outfit he'd liked best yesterday, the business, the casual or the sexy one. His eyes had seemed to caress her no matter what she'd worn.

Double damn him.

As Kelly sat up in the double bed in Wade's guest room, she marveled at her extraordinary thoughts. Was she really changing so much that she planned to make another move on the guy? More likely she was simply allowing her real self to come out of hiding. The notion both pleased and scared her, and made her think she might have more in common with Andrew than she'd thought. Perhaps going slowly and feeling her way into a relationship with

Wade would be prudent. On the other hand, she'd known him for years.

While she could still recall Cara's warnings about the dangerous Wade Lansing, her friend didn't know the man raised orchids. Or read books. Or acted the perfect gentleman. Besides, that edge of danger added a spark of excitement to their exchanges. She never quite knew what he would do next.

She sighed and padded to the bathroom. Last night, before she'd slipped under the covers, she'd called her parents and told them she wouldn't be home just yet. She'd rinsed out her underwear and hung them up to dry. Only, they were still damp and she couldn't bring herself to wear them. So she used the new toothbrush Wade had provided and donned her shirt and jeans.

Following her nose into the kitchen and the scent of perking coffee, she stepped over to the table. Wade sat tilted back on the rear legs of his chair, reading his newspaper. The moment he spied her, he put down the *Mustang Gazette* and leaned forward, his full attention almost making her self-conscious. He took in her finger-brushed hair and the slight bruise under her eye, and then his gaze swept over her chest, his pupils dilating slightly.

So, he'd noticed her lack of underwear. Served him right. She hoped naughty thoughts sucked the moisture right out of his mouth.

She grinned at him. "Morning."

"Morning."

Whether his voice was usually this husky in the morning or due to her lack of attire, she couldn't say. Pleased with herself, she walked over to the

kitchen counter. ''Can I have some coffee or are you
going to hog it all to yourself?''

He ducked his head back into the newspaper.
''Mugs are in the cabinet to the left of the sink.''

He might be pretending to read, but she knew her
braless state had thrown him, and swallowed down
another smile. While she hadn't gone without underwear to distract him, she couldn't have planned
better if she'd laid out a seduction campaign.

She filled a mug and sat across the table from him.
He handed her the local section and they sat together
reading like an old married couple. Well, not quite.
Going by her parents' marriage, married people
didn't usually have this kind of sexual tension hum-
ming between them, especially this early in the
morning.

The coffee chased away the last of her sleepiness.
''I'd like to ride out again today and see Debbie
West, her family and her ranch.''

''Well, we can't take my truck.'' Was that a blush
creeping up his neck? ''It's either your Jag or...''

''Or?'' she prodded, curious about the color in his
face.

''The Caddy.''

''You have a Cadillac?''

''I inherited Betsy from my uncle. Actually, Betsy
was his wife's car. After she died, he couldn't part
with it. And I've kept the car in storage all these
years, but she runs just fine.''

He didn't squirm in his seat, but he most definitely
fidgeted. A man who grew orchids in his kitchen and
was nostalgic over an old car—who would have
thought Wade capable of such sentimentality?

She savored the jolt of her morning caffeine and asked, "What aren't you telling me?"

"If we take Betsy, we won't be going incognito. She was built in 1955."

"Oh."

"And my aunt painted her hot pink."

"Wait a second. Isn't that the same car that used to be on the roof of the Hit 'Em Again?" She recalled the ridiculous pink car with the passion-purple banners and balloons that had been a Mustang Valley landmark for the better part of her childhood.

"Yeah." He grinned. "But the city inspectors made us take Betsy down. They said the car could fall on someone. Mayor Daniels probably just thought old Betsy was ugly."

"I didn't know you were so sentimental."

"I'm not."

"Whatever you say."

He scowled at her. "Stop that."

"What?" She kept her eyes wide and, hopefully, innocent looking.

His mouth curled upward in one of his irresistible bad-boy smiles that she couldn't help but find charming. "How can I argue with you if you stubbornly insist on agreeing with me?"

She raised her coffee cup to him in a toast. "You've made your point. But if you think that wisecrack remark is going to get me to agree with everything you say, then you don't know me very well."

"I know you better than you think."

"Really?"

"I know that you have a much better brain than

most people give you credit for. And while you take pleasure in your fashion-plate clothing, substance is more important to you than image.''

''What else?'' Her curiosity burned. What woman could resist hearing what a guy thought of her—especially a man who'd known her for years? A guy that was sending he-was-interested-but-wasn't-going-to-do-anything-about-it signals. A guy who had a reputation of playing fast and loose with other women, but who backpedaled away from her. They'd never been close, but she'd always been underfoot, and while she wasn't stunned by his perception, she was surprised that he'd turned the conversation so personal.

''You have determination and courage but wrap it all up in such a tidy, feminine package, you don't intimidate men who should feel threatened.''

''Men like you?'' she asked, recalling once again how he'd refused to join her in the hot tub. That he could refuse her at all rankled. And not because she couldn't take rejection, but because she couldn't ignore his blatant interest followed by resistance to her. Couldn't ignore his cool gray eyes meeting hers so frequently. Couldn't ignore the pleasure his hands had given her neck during his too-short massage. His interest was obvious, jolting and oh, so delicious—and yet she wanted to smack him upside the head for refusing to acknowledge where they were headed.

She felt as though she was three steps ahead of him. And not only had he no intention of keeping up, but he kept lagging further and further behind.

''Women like you scare the hell out of me,'' he

admitted with a bold grin that said just the opposite. "Now I suggest you stop fishing for compliments and get ready. Are we taking the Caddy or your Jag?"

She dug into her purse and pulled out her keys. "I think I'd like to be in the driver's seat today."

WADE SUSPECTED Kelly was irritated with him. However, he didn't expect her to turn up the music, then ignore him for the entire half-hour drive to the Wests' ranch. If she'd been a man, she would have been brooding. He preferred to think of her giving him the silent treatment as pouting. Pouting because she hadn't gotten her way.

Tough.

Kelly might be smart and courageous but she was also one very spoiled piece of work. He'd always thought she was a happily-ever-after kind of woman who wouldn't indulge in a fling. He'd been wrong, since her current behavior had proved otherwise. However, he didn't feel like letting her use him to scratch an itch with the town's bad boy during her summer break before she returned to law school and forgot all about him. Nope. Wade knew better than to knuckle under and give her what she so obviously wanted.

Not that he wouldn't enjoy making love to her. He would have enjoyed it immensely. Just the thought of him being the one to draw soft moans of pleasure from her throat, of skimming his hands over her silky, pliant flesh, of finally tasting those sultry lips could heat him hotter than sizzling oil in a hot skillet.

But the thought of her exploiting him held him back. She only had one use for a man like him, and if he gave her what she wanted, he wouldn't just be going back on an implied promise to Andrew, he would be selling himself short. Just because she might require comforting to help her get past the loss of her brother, didn't mean that Wade would let her trample his own esteem in the process. His blood might not come from the illustrious Shotgun Sally of McGovern fame, but he had his standards—ones that most definitely didn't include Ms. Kelly Mc-Govern.

So he let her drive and sulk. Let her stay miffed with his refusal to play the dating game.

He tipped his hat over his closed eyes and pretended to sleep, but surreptitiously he kept checking the side-view mirror. No menacing tow trucks appeared on the highway. This road was as clear as the morning air without a cloud in sight.

Wade had never been to the Wests' homestead before. But the overgrazed forty acres didn't appear much different from the other mom-and-pop ranches that were all slowly going out of business throughout the West. The little guys couldn't compete with the large corporations that used all the newest technology, who herded cattle by helicopter and bought in volume and were managed by a team of agricultural experts.

Kelly slowed down considerably before turning onto the dirt drive, which nevertheless shot up choking dust. She shut off the engine, but neither made a move to exit until the dust settled. Outside, the bright sun glared and he kept his sunglasses on.

Kelly did the same. He saw her taking in the yard overgrown with weeds, the peeling paint on the sagging front porch, the curling and worn shingles on a lumpy roof.

The air smelled of sweat, dirt and manure from the cows behind the barbwire fence. Two rusty bikes, both with flat tires, and an old wheelbarrow rotted next to a barn that had been old twenty years ago. He didn't blame the Wests for selling their ranch. Surely they could do better elsewhere than this overbaked piece of dirt.

Kelly stood still for a moment, taking in the poor land, ignoring the buzzing flies. Looking as out of place as a fairy princess in a sweatshop, she nevertheless squared her shoulders and headed up the front porch steps. Clearly, she didn't want to be here, but true to form, she would press on until she had the answers she sought.

He admired grit in a woman, but wished she'd confided in him. He had no idea if the Wests would welcome them or not. The few times he'd met Debbie, she'd been with Andrew, who tended to overshadow her. And the only time he'd seen Debbie and Kelly together had been at Andrew's funeral where they'd kept their distance from each another.

A barking dog announced their presence, but Kelly rapped smartly on the front door, anyway. Still giving him the silent treatment, she didn't even glance his way.

With one hand wrapped in the pit bull's collar, Debbie opened the door. She wore a tank top, cutoff jeans and her hair tied back in a bandanna. No shoes. Her chestnut hair was streaked with dust, cobwebs and grime. But her eyes, dark with sorrow and puffy from too many tears, told of her misery and revealed her surprise to see them.

"Hey, come in." She shoved a rag into her pocket and tugged the barking dog back inside. "I was just cleaning the windows."

The inside of the ranch house had cheap tile floors that were immaculate. A threadbare carpet lay in front of a worn sofa. However, the coffee table gleamed with a silver tea set and white doilies. And not by one twitch of her lips or change of expression in her blue eyes did Kelly reveal that she was unaccustomed to these kinds of surroundings. In fact, if he hadn't known her better, he would have sworn that she was as comfortable here as she had been at his place.

He wondered why he found her adaptability so surprising when Andrew had exhibited the same trait. Wade supposed he made those assumptions about Kelly because of her clothes that always had a style that set her apart, that said, "I'm special." And he'd been fooled by her airs and her outfits like just about everyone else in town, except Cara. He should have realized the brash and smart reporter had befriended Kelly for her inner qualities—qualities he couldn't help admiring as much as he did the more visible ones.

"Would you like some sweet tea?" Debbie asked, offering Southern hospitality that would have been rude to refuse. "I just made some this morning."

"Thanks." Kelly fearlessly held out her hand to let the pit bull have a sniff, then slowly patted the dog on the head. "What's his name?"

"Brutus." Debbie stepped into the kitchen, placed a pitcher of tea on a tray next to mismatched glasses with ice, then carried everything to the living room. "If you know anyone who might want him, we need to give him away before we move. He's a great watchdog and he's never bitten anyone. I can't keep him with me at the new apartment."

"So you're definitely selling?" Kelly asked, her tone casual, but Wade sensed she would soon come to the real reason for their visit.

"I have a job in town." Debbie settled in a chair next to her dog. "With the mayor. I'm working for city hall. He wants me to liaise with the ranchers and farming community."

"That's great." Kelly crossed her legs and folded her feet under the sofa, seeming genuinely happy for Debbie. "And your father?"

"The mayor's offered to find him a job, too—if he can stay sober." Debbie poured the iced tea. "Andrew set up the sale of this ranch as well as the new jobs for us before he died."

"That's why we came," Kelly spoke gently. "Are you up to talking about Andrew?"

Debbie's eyes narrowed on Kelly. "I suppose."

"Did Andrew have any enemies that you know about?" Wade asked. Although he knew Kelly was perfectly capable of asking the right questions, there was a tension between the two women, almost as if Andrew were still alive and they were fighting over him.

Debbie's sharp gaze sliced to Wade, then back to Kelly. She set down her tea and folded her arms over her chest. "What's this all about?"

"Yesterday Kelly and I were asking a lot of questions around town about Andrew," Wade explained. "On our way here, a stolen truck ran us off the road. My truck was totaled. We think someone tried to kill us."

Debbie's eyebrows arched. "Because you were asking questions about Andrew?"

"Yes." Kelly also set down her practically untouched tea. "If there's anything you can tell us, I'd be grateful."

By unspoken agreement, neither Kelly nor Wade wanted to tell Debbie that Andrew had been murdered. She or her ex-husband could be connected to the killing and if so, Wade didn't want her leaving town—not before they figured out what was going on. Since she had no motive, Wade didn't believe Debbie had anything to do with Andrew's murder, but she could have accidentally given information to someone else who did.

"Well, Niles, my ex-husband has hated Andrew since Andrew and I got together. Andrew's handling of our divorce didn't help."

"Exactly how angry was Niles?" Kelly asked, and by her tone Wade could tell she hated prying.

Debbie sighed. "Niles has a temper, but he's not usually violent—if that's what you're asking—and I've never known him to get his hands dirty."

She left the statement hanging. Kelly and Wade knew that Niles had the funds to hire people to do his dirty work.

"Anyone else?" Wade asked. "What about your father? Did he and Andrew get along?"

"At first Daddy wasn't too keen about Andrew,

but after he did such a good job negotiating the sale of our land to those big lawyers, Daddy changed his thinking. Andrew got us a better price and a faster closing date.''

"Did my brother ever mention any clients who were angry with him?'' Kelly asked.

"Not really.'' Debbie frowned and then pressed her lips firmly together as if remembering something she didn't want to reveal.

"What is it?'' Wade asked.

"Probably nothing.''

"Can you please tell us anyway?'' Kelly prodded.

"Andrew asked me never to repeat it…but… Promise me that you won't tell anyone else?''

Wade nodded. "I promise—unless it turns out that this person is trying to kill us—then our deal is off.''

"Fair enough.'' Debbie picked up her tea, drained half the glass in two gulps, then twisted the tumbler in her hands. "During Andrew's last year in law school, he was involved in an unpleasant incident.''

Wade glanced at Kelly, who shook her head, indicating she knew nothing about what Debbie was about to reveal. Neither did Wade.

Debbie sighed again. "Andrew saw another student cheating on a final exam. Now, the code of honor at law school made him duty bound to report the cheater, but Andrew didn't want to. He knew that his coming forward would cause the other student to be expelled, and likely the cheater would never attain his law degree.''

"Andrew must have been torn up over that decision,'' Kelly muttered.

Her brother, always the rooter for the underdog, would hate to end another person's career before it had begun. And yet Andrew's personal code of honor wouldn't allow for cheaters, either.

"What did Andrew do?" Wade asked, his gut already churning because he knew his friend well enough to know the decision must have given him many sleepless nights.

"He turned Jonathan Dixon in. Sure enough, the school expelled the man two weeks before graduation. And it's a good thing Andrew turned him in, because the professor had also seen the man cheating and suspected Andrew also knew. If Andrew had kept quiet, he too could have been expelled for failing to report the incident."

"Jonathan blamed Andrew?" Kelly guessed.

"What do you think?" Debbie downed the rest of her tea. "It got ugly. Jonathan issued threats, and the campus police had to physically remove him from the classroom. But you know Andrew. Instead of being angry for being put in that awkward position, he wanted to help the guy. So he told Jonathan that if he ever needed a job, to come to Mustang Valley and look him up."

Kelly groaned, clearly annoyed that her brother had tried to befriend someone who might be dangerous—which was probably why Andrew hadn't mentioned the incident to either Wade or Kelly. Both of them would certainly have advised him to just forget the unpleasant episode and move on. Some people couldn't be helped, but Andrew had never seemed to understand that. Odd how he and Kelly thought alike on the matter.

Kelly kept her tone neutral. "And this Jonathan, did he come to Mustang Valley?"

Debbie nodded. "Andrew got him a job working for the mayor, too."

"When?" Wade asked.

"The week before Andrew died."

*A week?* Now that was a huge coincidence that needed looking into.

"Seems like the mayor is in a hiring mood," Wade commented, his thoughts churning. Mustang Valley had been growing large enough that he didn't necessarily recognize every stranger in the Hit 'Em Again Saloon. And city hall was growing by leaps and bounds. Between Daniels's reelection campaign and the growth of Mustang Valley, Wade supposed the city employed quite a few people, who all technically worked for the mayor. But Wade still knew most people in town, and, as far as he knew, Jonathan had yet to frequent his establishment.

"Jonathan's job is only temporary. Just until the election. Andrew was trying to line up something else for him for afterward." Debbie sighed. "I have to tell you that Jonathan seems like a really nice man. I can't imagine him stealing a tow truck and trying to run you down."

Kelly frowned. "Wade told you that the tow truck ran us off the road, not tried to run us down."

Debbie shrugged. "Same difference."

But was her wording an assumption? Or did she know more than she was telling? And what about her Jonathan story? Was that to throw them off track? It seemed suspicious that someone who had a motive for revenge had shown up in town a week before Andrew's death.

"Oh, I almost forgot. Jonathan is going by the name of Johnny. He claims he wants to make a new start."

"Johnny?" Facts clicked in Wade's mind. "Is Johnny about five-six with black hair and a mustache?"

Debbie's eyes widened. "You know him?"

"Yeah. He's been in for a few drinks." Wade rubbed his knuckles in recollection of the last time Johnny had a few too many. When Johnny turned surly and obnoxious, Wade had cut the man off and Johnny had staggered from the bar, furious. He'd slammed into another customer and a brawl had broken out. Six broken chairs and one cracked mirror later, Wade had thrown out the drunk and restored order.

Johnny hadn't returned again.

Wade didn't find it odd that Andrew hadn't introduced him. But he did find Kelly's accusing eyes on him uncomfortable. He hadn't said a word, but she seemed to know he was holding back. Yet she clearly understood that he didn't want to say more in front of Debbie and gave him a slow nod and a we'll-talk-later look.

Who would have thought the bartender and the debutante could work so well together? Almost like a team.

# Chapter Six

"Mom. Daddy?" Kelly walked through the front door of her home with Wade beside her. The stubborn man had insisted on sticking to her like mascara. Unlike her makeup, she couldn't just wash him away. So she was forced to make explanations to her parents, which she never found easy, with Wade right there to hear every word. Why did men and parents have to be so difficult? "I'm home."

"Don't shout, dear. We're in the breakfast room."

Kelly checked her makeup in the foyer mirror, smoothed lip gloss that didn't need smoothing with her pinky and enjoyed the fact that Wade stood there trying to look patient and unable to look away. Just for spite, she fluffed her hair, knowing it would both annoy and fascinate him, then swallowed down a grin. Seemed she did that a lot around Wade.

Annoyed that he'd refused to stay in her car while she picked up a few changes of clothes and some necessities, she entered the breakfast room with trepidation. Her mother had recently painted the walls a rich burgundy, and contrasted the woodwork trim with a creamy white that supposedly encouraged dining enjoyment by setting the right tone. The octagonal airy space with windows overlooking the garden was usually one of Kelly's favorite rooms. In fact, her folks often ate informal dinners there as they were doing right now, but today she dreaded going inside.

After Andrew's death, she didn't want to cause her parents any more pain by having them worry over their remaining offspring. And knowing Mustang Valley's gossip network as well as she did, by now half the town had either spied her driving with Wade or had actually seen them together and reported it to friends, co-workers and family.

However, she'd loved her brother way too much not to seek justice. She wanted to put behind bars the person who'd murdered him. She wanted his killer to pay for his crime, and if that made her as bloodthirsty as Shotgun Sally, then so be it.

Her parents had to know she'd been keeping company with Wade, and they wouldn't be pleased— less pleased if they knew what kind of trouble she'd stirred up. Trying to make the best of an awkward situation, she pasted a cheery grin on her face, looped her arm through Wade's and escorted him to meet her parents.

Of course, they'd all met before through Andrew. But Daddy wouldn't be happy to see her hanging out with the man he derogatorily called the saloon keeper, and Mom wouldn't necessarily back Kelly up. But then again, she might. Like all the women in the McGovern family back to Shotgun Sally, Mom had a mind of her own and she could be ever so unpredictable.

"Mom. Daddy. I brought Wade over, and we don't have time for dinner." Kelly leaned over and kissed her father on the cheek. He raised his smooth, aristocratic cheek to her, but his dark hazel eyes were shadowed with concern.

Her mother, a petite blonde with Kelly's blue eyes, stood and took two plates out of the china cabinet and set additional silverware. "Of course you'll eat. We're going to sit down together like a family and have a discussion."

"Yes, dear." Her father agreed, nodding his head with a firmness that told Kelly they might even know more than she'd suspected.

She and Wade were about to be ganged up on with all the Southern politeness that should have had them running in the opposite direction. But leaving without making some explanations wasn't an option, though she felt like a child who had done something wrong and was about to be scolded and punished.

"Sit down. Have some steak." Her father passed the platter to Wade.

"Thank you, sir."

"Serving you dinner is the least I can do since you're protecting my little girl."

*Protecting?* Uh-oh. She shot her mom a how-much-do-you-know look.

Her mother rolled her eyes at the ceiling. Obviously, Kelly had really underestimated them this time. To say her mother was smart was an understatement. She could complete the *New York Times* crossword puzzle in thirty minutes flat. Daddy always consulted her on his oil deals, and Kelly suspected her mother could have run the company better than he did.

Not that Daddy didn't do a fine job. But like Andrew, he tended to see the good side of people and overlooked the bad, and she loved him for it. Besides, as a good family man, when it came to protecting his loved ones, he could be ferocious.

Kelly filled her plate with char-grilled steak, shoestring French fries and jalepeño stuffed olives. Her father poured them both a goblet of rich Bordeaux, then set the crystal wine decanter on the white linen tablecloth without spilling a drop.

Her mother passed the salad. ''We know Andrew was murdered.''

They knew? Kelly almost dropped the platter her mother was handing her.

She and Wade exchanged glances, and he subtly shrugged, which she took to mean as, this is your family, I'll let you handle them. Great. She'd always avoided confrontations by doing pretty much what her parents wanted. Early on, her idea of rebellion had been to carry lipstick and eye shadow in her purse and apply the cosmetics after she left the house for school. So she was accustomed to her parents' approval and disliked causing discord. And deep down she knew that they wouldn't be pleased with her spending time with Wade looking into Andrew's murder or for putting herself in danger.

Normally she might have obeyed their wishes, but Andrew was too important to her to let the comment slide. His loss had shaken her safe world in a manner that had her questioning her life, her values, her goals. First and foremost in her mind was getting

Andrew some justice, and she no longer knew if she wanted to attend law school, when staying in Mustang Valley near her parents, her friends and Wade seemed much more appealing. At least she needn't make that decision right now.

"Sheriff Wilson told Mayor Daniels, who then told me." Her father sliced his steak, but didn't raise the meat to his mouth. "Your mother and I wanted to keep the news from you because we feared you'd go looking into Andrew's death and put yourself in danger."

"Which is exactly what you've done," her mother said with both vexation and sympathy. "Did you think we wouldn't hear about that stolen tow truck almost running you down?"

"I never could keep secrets from you guys," Kelly muttered. "I only tried because I didn't want you to worry."

"We're always going to worry about you," her mother said.

"I'm not a little girl anymore."

"Age has nothing to do with it. I'll worry about you when you're sixty." Her mother paused, her eyes tearing, then she regained control of herself and continued. "Andrew was our son and we loved him very much. The pain of losing him will never go away. Never. It'll be there whether we talk about him or not. It'll be there whether we find out who killed him or not." Her mother dabbed at her tearing eyes with a napkin. "And we don't want to lose you, too. I just couldn't bear it if anything else happens to this family."

Fresh guilt stabbed Kelly and made her stomach

quiver. "Mom, I could stop asking questions right now—"

"But it's too late for that," Wade said, inserting himself into the family conversation. "I don't believe Kelly will be safe—not until we find out what happened to Andrew."

"We agree." Her mother reached across the table and squeezed her father's hand. "That's why we want to send both of you out of town."

"Both of us?" Kelly's pulse pounded with uncertainty. She'd always thought that her parents hadn't liked Wade, hadn't liked Andrew hanging out with him. Then she realized that they thought of Wade as protection for her. They didn't know that she liked him in other, not so simple, ways.

"We don't want you to be alone," her father said, confirming her suspicions, and she did nothing to clear up their misconception.

Her mother outlined their plan. "We'll hire a private investigator—"

"That won't work and you know it, Mom." Kelly picked up a stuffed olive and popped it into her mouth, chewed and swallowed, giving her time to form her reply. "People in Mustang Valley don't talk to outsiders."

Her father frowned. "Our first priority is *your* safety."

"Look, if someone wants me dead and I leave, who's to say they won't follow me?" Her parents traded a long glance, and she could see they were worried about that possibility, too. "Besides, if I'm in danger, I'd rather be on my home ground with friends around me I can trust. Seems to me the best way for me to be safe is to find Andrew's killer and turn him or her over to the authorities."

Her father gave up all pretense of eating, threw down his napkin and shoved his chair back from the table. "Have you thought of giving the sheriff time to do his job?"

"If he hasn't found anything by now, he probably won't." Wade kept his tone even and firm, but he sure didn't seem to mind standing up to her father, which she appreciated, especially since he did it respectfully. "And I don't trust the sheriff."

She thought her father might rant. That he might throw Wade's background in his face for not believing the law would help. But Daddy surprised her.

He swirled his wine in his glass, then shot a piercing stare at Wade. "Why don't you trust Wilson?"

Wade held her father's stare. "Our sheriff's more concerned with the mayor's reelection campaign than in solving Andrew's murder."

"Is that your only reason?" her father asked.

"Yes, sir." Wade hesitated, as if choosing his words very carefully. "That's the only reason I'm willing to state out loud."

"SO THEN WHAT HAPPENED?" Cara asked while the two friends met in the reporter's office the following day at the *Mustang Gazette*.

Kelly sighed. "We finished dinner without coming to any agreement. When we left the house Mom looked ready to burst into tears again and Dad looked...defeated. They want me to leave Mustang Valley, but I'm not going."

"Good. So what's next?"

''Wade had to order supplies for his saloon and pay a few bills. He dropped me off here, escorted me to your door and made me promise not to leave until he returns. We're going to check out Jonathan Dixon, the guy who cheated in law school and now works for the mayor. Then we may head to Dallas, if Niles Deagen will talk to us.''

''Niles Deagen? The oil man?''

''And Debbie's secret ex-husband.''

From behind her desk, Cara started typing on her keyboard. ''I've got a file on him. Last year I was researching a story about oil and his name came up.''

Kelly came around Cara's desk and peered over her friend's shoulder at the monitor. ''You have anything interesting?''

''Depends what you mean by interesting. I have Deagen's home phone number and the address of his last lover.'' Cara used her mouse. ''Here it is. I'll print out the file.'' While they waited for the printer to spit out the information, Cara drummed her nails on her desk.

Kelly recalled going through Andrew's box of stuff last night. Nothing seemed sinister, but the mayor's campaign literature she found reminded her that Jonathan needed watching. Any guy that tried to cheat his way through law school obviously didn't have good character. While cheating on a test was very different from murder, she felt Jonathan was their best lead.

''Do you have any information on the mayor?'' Kelly asked.

''Like what?''

"His scheduled speeches and campaign agenda might help us track down Jonathan without asking too many questions and drawing more attention to ourselves." Kelly checked her watch, wishing they had more time to chat. "Wade should be here soon."

"Hold on and you can have the mayor's stuff, too."

"Thanks, Cara. Oh, yeah, I almost forgot. When Wade and I were over at Lambert & Church, Lindsey Wellington told us that Andrew had a client who wasn't satisfied with my brother's representation after he lost custody of his kids."

"That would have been Sean McCardel."

"Yes. Does he still live in Mustang Valley?"

"I have no idea but I'll pull up the *Mustang Gazette's* articles about him. And while we wait for the printouts, why don't you tell me more about what's going on between you and Wade."

Had Kelly just wished for more time? Suddenly she couldn't wait for Wade to arrive.

Kelly liked having parents and friends who were concerned about her—at least most of the time. This wasn't one of them. Especially since last night had been a complete disaster. Wade had spent the entire evening trying to talk her into hiding while he tried to solve Andrew's murder alone. His chauvinistic attitude had riled Kelly's normally easy-going nature.

Kelly's voice came out sharper than she intended. "Must you always be the inquisitive reporter?"

"I thought I was being the inquisitive friend,"

Cara snapped, her temper clearly simmering, but her eyes showing Kelly's unthinking remark had hurt.

"Damn, I'm sorry. Really, sorry. I shouldn't take out my frustration on you."

"No problem." Cara's eyes softened with sympathy. "You've been through a lot."

Kelly realized that, as much as she tried to tell herself that her life was still normal, she was stressed out and had every right to be. She'd lost her brother. Someone had tried to kill her, and she and Wade...there was no "she and Wade." "After I fought with my folks, Wade and I argued. Or rather he lectured and I refused to listen."

"I take it you didn't end the fight by making mad, passionate love?"

"I wish." Kelly almost smiled at Cara's sarcasm. "That man is so stubborn that I want to smack him almost as often as I want to kiss him."

"Wow. You've got it bad. Maybe you should just take him to bed and work him out of your system."

"You don't understand."

"So educate me."

"He doesn't want me." At her admission, Cara's lower jaw dropped, and Kelly held up her hand before her friend could press for more information. "I take that back. He wants me. He just won't do anything about it."

"No wonder you're frustrated."

"I'll straighten myself out. I have a plan of sorts."

"So what are you going to do?"

Kelly saw Wade entering through the office door

and grinned at Cara, not caring if he overheard. "I'm planning a Shotgun Sally moment."

Cara signaled her with a thumbs-up. "You go, girl."

WADE WAITED until they were safely out of the *Mustang Gazette,* off the street and inside Kelly's Jaguar before letting loose his curiosity. Kelly had this just-swallowed-a-rich-creamy-chocolate look on her face, and it stayed with her as they'd said goodbye to Cara and exited the building.

He strapped on his seat belt, glad he wasn't driving so he could study Kelly's face. "What's a Shotgun Sally moment?"

"My ancestor had her own ways of dealing with men." Kelly slipped on a pair of sunglasses, put the Jag into gear and merged with Main Street's traffic. "She was a real aristocratic widow lady who ran a saloon for a few years. She stored a shotgun behind the bar, but she kept all those rowdy men in line without ever taking down the gun."

"That's hard to believe." Wade had run the saloon since he was eighteen years old and was skeptical of a genteel lady keeping order among a bunch of wild cowboys, especially more than a century ago when times were even rougher. "But maybe the men were more chivalrous back then. Still, a drunk is a drunk, and most have no manners."

She pushed the sunglasses high up on her nose. "Legend says Sally only fired her shotgun once. And that was a warning shot to keep her lover Zachary Gale from trying to run away from his promise to marry her."

"And this is a woman you admire?"

"Absolutely. She's a woman who knew what she wanted and wasn't afraid to go after it. Since Sally didn't have a father to make Zachary live up to his word, she did the reminding herself."

Kelly seemed to find the legend amusing. Either that or she had something else in mind. Something she intended to keep secret, and he wasn't sure how he felt about that. On the one hand he didn't expect her to tell him every thought in her head. On the other, he didn't like her holding back on him, either.

That he was worried about what she was thinking when he should have his mind on solving Andrew's murder told him she was getting to him. Despite the sunglasses that hid her vivid blue eyes, and the way she didn't seem to want to share what was on her mind, he suspected her Shotgun Sally moment had something to do with him.

What was she planning? Obviously, she wouldn't tell him until she was good and ready.

So he picked on Shotgun Sally to test Kelly's patience, just as she was testing his. "If Sally had to force Zachary to marry her, he couldn't have been much of a catch."

"Oh, he was," Kelly insisted. "Zach just didn't like commitment or the idea of giving up his freedom—at least that's what my grandmother told me, and she heard the story from her grandmother."

Wade chuckled. "Seems to me the ladies in your family may have romanticized things."

"Sally was just being practical. She was pregnant and the baby needed a father." Kelly defended her ancestor with a zest that made him believe her enthusiasm wasn't so much about the story she told but about her planned Shotgun Sally moment—whatever that was.

A flying rock, followed by the sound of shattering glass caught Wade's attention. He glimpsed kids fleeing the damaged storefront. "Turn left at the corner."

Kelly frowned, but steered the car as he directed. "But campaign headquarters are—"

"I know where they are. I just saw a couple of kids throwing rocks."

Kelly kept going, but mumbled something about having better things to do than chase down a few juvenile delinquents. But Wade thought he'd recognized a certain tattered green backpack on a skinny kid with short black hair.

The Jag turned the corner and the boys split into three directions. "Stop the car."

Wade unsnapped his seat belt, opened the door and set off through the park at top speed. It took him a full sixty seconds at a flat-out run to catch the kid by his backpack and shove him up against the wall.

Wade pushed his face right at the kid's. "Damn it, Rudy. Are you part of the group that threw rocks at the doc's place, too? What the hell do you think you're doing?"

"Nothing."

"You call throwing rocks nothing?"

Rudy shrugged. "You gonna let me go or not?"

"Not." Wade gripped his shoulder, hard enough to make Rudy wince. "We're going back to that store. You're going to apologize and work off the damage you did."

"And if I don't?" The son of Wade's dishwasher shouted with defiance, but Rudy was trembling so hard that Wade knew he was a hair's breadth from bursting into tears. Rudy wasn't a bad kid, but he hung out with the wrong crowd. While Wade wanted to give him a break, he knew the kid had to take responsibility for his actions.

Rudy drew his skinny shoulders back straight, waiting for Wade's answer.

And of course Wade knew the kid wasn't half as scared of the law as he was of his parents. So he spoke mildly. "Then I'll just have to tell your father."

The kid caved. His shoulders sagged and the fire went out of his eyes just as Kelly came running up, her eyes worried. "What happened?"

Rudy took one look at Kelly and his eyes turned crafty. "I'll make you another deal instead."

Wade yanked him toward the broken window. "You're in no position to bargain."

"The lady might think otherwise."

"Do I know you?" Kelly peered at Rudy. In his baggy jeans and overly large T-shirt, he looked younger than his fourteen years. But Wade doubted they'd met.

"This is Rudy Waters. His father works for me."

"I know you," Rudy spoke up with a determination that surprised Wade. "You're Kelly McGovern, and your brother got himself murdered—at least that's what the sheriff told the mayor."

Wade didn't think the kid was making up lies to save himself. Unlike his hardworking father, Rudy habitually sneaked out, but the kid liked to eavesdrop. Wade had caught him doing so several times in the Hit 'Em Again's pool hall. From experience, he knew that people never paid attention to what they said around kids.

"What else did the sheriff say?" Wade demanded.

"If I tell, you'll let me go?"

Wade reached into his pocket, pulled out his wallet and slipped out a few bills as if he was going to pay Rudy. "Depends on what you have to say."

"The sheriff told the mayor that Kelly McGovern was stirring up trouble, and if she wasn't careful she might get herself killed."

Kelly's eyes went round. Wade shook his head slightly, signaling for her to remain silent.

Rudy shook off Wade's hand on his shoulder and tried to snag the cash.

Wade pulled the money just out of reach of Rudy's fingertips. "What else?"

Rudy eyed the bills hungrily but dropped his hand to his side. "Ain't that enough?"

Wade tried to draw out more information from the kid. "When the sheriff was talking did he sound worried or did he sound like he was making a threat?"

The kid hesitated as if deciding which answer would earn him the money faster.

Wade shook his shoulder. "I want the truth."

"I don't know." Rudy's voice was surly. "They kept their voices way low."

"Where did you hear this conversation?"

"At the mayor's headquarters."

Wade wished they had more to go on. The sheriff's remark could have been perfectly innocent. The man could be legitimately worried over Kelly's safety, especially after the tow-truck incident yesterday. And then again, his words could also have more sinister implications. Either way, Wade didn't have time to fool with Rudy.

"This money is to pay for the window you broke." Wade stuffed the money into the boy's hand, grateful the broken pane had been a small side panel of glass and not the main one. "Now go pay for the damage. We'll be watching."

"Wait." Kelly stopped the boy. "If you hear anything else I might be interested in, you come to me and I'll reward you for your time. Understand?"

Wade's admiration for Kelly spiked up another notch. She hadn't interfered with his holding the kid against the wall. She'd kept her mouth shut at the right time. Yet she might have gained them a snoop, one whom no one would suspect.

He only hoped that the boy's avaricious nature didn't put him in danger. But Rudy was a street-smart kid and would protect himself first and foremost. He knew how to stay really quiet so that people didn't notice him. And if he'd been hanging out around campaign headquarters, his presence there a second time wouldn't be suspicious.

Rudy licked his lips greedily. "Yeah, lady. I understand. You're in even more trouble than me."

# Chapter Seven

*Think positive.*

Kelly tried to put the kid's words out of her mind as Wade opened the door to Mayor Daniels's campaign headquarters for her. Red-white-and-blue banners, buttons, posters and literature dominated the formerly unleased storefront. Inside, a surprising amount of activity hummed. Three people manned phone banks. A fax machine spat out paper. A man ran copies and a group of women congregated around a coffeepot in a makeshift kitchen.

A kid like Rudy wouldn't have been noticed among all the bustle, and his words haunted Kelly. Had he been telling the truth? Kids exaggerated. Yet ever since he'd mentioned the sheriff and the mayor's discussion, she'd felt unsettled. Even Wade's teasing her about Shotgun Sally on the ride over hadn't distracted her from the possibility that Andrew might have been involved in something that other people didn't want known. Something for which he'd been murdered.

"It's hard to tell who's in charge." Wade walked

over to a woman wearing a button that read Vote for Daniels.

The harried redhead looked up with bleary eyes from the newspaper ads spread out on a folding table and appeared to recognize that they didn't belong here. As if on cue, she smiled politely. "Hi. I'm Rebecca. Are you two here to deliver flyers?"

Wade kept his voice low. "We're looking for Jonathan, Johnny Dixon. Is he around?"

Rebecca shook her head. "He didn't come in today."

"Do you know where we can find him?" Kelly asked.

"Not only is Johnny absent today, he didn't call, either." Rebecca frowned. "And that's not like him."

"Ma'am, do you have his phone number or home address?" Wade asked.

"I'm sorry. I can't give out that kind of information. However, if you'd like to leave a message, I'll give it to Johnny when he arrives."

Mayor Daniels walked out of the back room, and the flurry of activity in the room heightened as everyone busied themselves. At fifty, his signature gray hair and friendly green eyes had won him many votes. Popular with both the townsfolk and the ranchers, the mayor would likely be reelected for the fourth time.

He stuck out his hand to welcome Kelly. To add warmth, he clasped his other hand over hers, too.

Kelly didn't know if the combination of sympathy and warmth in his eyes was genuine, but played along as if he was an old friend of the family. In truth, she didn't know the mayor well. But her daddy did, and Daniels had been at Andrew's funeral with most of the other of Mustang Valley's leading citizens.

"Welcome, Kelly."

Rebecca left them with the mayor and returned to sorting newspaper ads. Mayor Daniels shook Wade's hand in the same friendly manner as he had hers. "Wade. Have you two come to volunteer for my campaign?"

"I'm afraid not." Kelly understood why the man was so good at his job. After she turned him down, he didn't show any disappointment. Instead he maintained the same expression as she continued, "But we could use your help."

"What can I do?" he offered, his lips narrowing just a bit.

"We're looking for an old friend of my brother Andrew's. Johnny Dixon."

"He's a great kid. Hard worker." Daniels peered around the room. "He doesn't seem to be here, but Rebecca can tell you where she's sent him."

"Rebecca just told us that he hasn't come in today," Wade said.

The mayor's eyes shifted from Wade to Kelly and back around the room, almost as if he were acting. She wondered if the mayor already knew that Johnny wasn't there, and wondered if he had any reason to lie.

Kelly leaned forward and touched the mayor's arm. "We were hoping you could give us his phone number and address." At the hesitation in his eyes she repeated, "Johnny was a friend of Andrew's."

"I know." The mayor lost his smile. "Andrew introduced us, but you aren't going to do anything dangerous, are you?"

"You heard about someone running us off the road yesterday?" Wade asked.

"Yeah. The sheriff doesn't think it was an accident, and we're both concerned about you two playing amateur detective. One unexplained death in this town is already one too many. Mustang Valley is a safe place, and we don't need a reputation for violence. It's not good for the residents or the corporations thinking about investing here, and it's not good for my campaign."

"Gee, Mayor. I'd hate to get myself murdered and hurt your campaign," Kelly muttered.

"Look, I didn't mean to sound that cold and you know it. I don't approve of you putting yourself in danger. Let the sheriff do his job."

He sounded concerned. But he was a polished politician, and his voice was probably trained as well as an actor's and could convey whatever he wished.

Kelly forced herself to keep her tone light. "I just wanted to talk to Johnny about law school. I've been accepted for fall semester."

Daniels's grin came back. "Congratulations."

Kelly wondered if his cheeks hurt from all his smiling or if the muscles were accustomed to it. At least she seemed to have turned the topic away from her investigating and the danger. "I'd always figured that Andrew would be around to show me the ropes, but…"

She let her sentence dangle in the air between them unfinished, feeling not the least bit guilty for misleading the man after almost dying yesterday. A girl had to do what a girl had to do. And right now, everyone was a suspect.

Wade put a protective arm over her shoulder. "You'll be fine."

The mayor headed for a file cabinet. "I guess Johnny won't mind my giving out his address to the sister of his old friend." He fingered through file tabs, stopped and read. "It's 22 Mustang Road. Apartment 1C. It's that brick building on the corner with the flat roof across from the gas station."

"Thanks. I know where it is." Wade offered his hand to Daniels.

Daniels shook it. "Johnny's phone number is under new listings in the phone book, but I'll save you the trouble." He wrote on a piece of notepaper and handed it over.

Kelly folded the paper and slipped it into her pocket. "Thank you so much."

"I hope you find what you're looking for." Daniels started to step away and then turned back. "And, Wade?"

"Yes, sir?"

Daniels's tone hardened. "Keep her out of the way of Sheriff Wilson's investigation."

"I'll try, sir."

Kelly smiled sweetly at the two men towering over her. "Did you two forget what century this is?"

"Huh?" Wade muttered.

"What are you saying?" Daniels asked.

"Women have voting rights these days," she pointed out.

Wade scowled at her. The mayor recovered more quickly. "Of course they do. I'll be counting on your vote."

WADE DIDN'T LIKE politicians. He supposed it had something to do with someone else earning a living off his hard-earned tax dollars. In addition, Daniels's smooth-talking ways irritated him. He couldn't read the man and therefore didn't trust him. Which probably meant that Daniels was simply very good at his job.

As they walked down the sidewalk back to her car, Kelly plucked from her purse the cell phone her parents had given her before she'd left their house. Wade didn't blame her folks for wanting to keep tabs on their daughter and reminded himself to replace his own ruined phone. Between keeping his business afloat during his absence and investigating Andrew's murder with Kelly, Wade hadn't had much free time. Nor did he have any family members to worry about him.

His mom had split when he was just a kid. His father had drunk himself into an early grave. An aunt and uncle had taken him in and tried to raise him but by then he'd been accustomed to complete freedom and doing things his way. He now regretted what a tough time he'd given them. After their deaths in a car accident, he'd inherited the Hit 'Em Again and that had probably saved him.

He'd been forced to take on the responsibility of running the business or lose the roof over his head. And he'd worked damn hard to make the place a success. At least he had a good manager to stand in for him. Since he hadn't taken off more than one day a week since he'd inherited the saloon, Wade figured he was due a vacation. If he chose to spend that time with Kelly, and check in once in a while, that was his call—one of the advantages of the self-employed.

Kelly unfolded the paper with Johnny's telephone number and dialed. She held the phone to her ear but didn't say a word for a minute, then snapped it shut with a sigh.

"No answer?" he asked.

She shook her head. "No answering machine or voice mail, either." Kelly plucked the car keys from her purse and tossed them to Wade. "Would you mind driving?"

He snatched the keys out of the air. "Yeah, it's such a chore to drive a Jaguar."

"Very funny."

She didn't wait for him to open her door for her but slipped into the plush leather seat and donned her seat belt. The lady had something on her mind and he couldn't quite peg her mood. Was she considering the mayor's suggestion that they quit? He didn't think so. Ever since she'd left Cara and the *Mustang Gazette,* her temperament had been...pensive.

She didn't even ask him where he was driving, but since they had a little time to kill until they tried Johnny's phone number again, he headed out of town, leaving the traffic behind. He drove past suburban areas until the houses were farther and farther apart and they finally headed onto a dirt road. When he stopped to open a barbwire gate, she seemed to come out of her trance. To open the gate, he slipped out of the Jag before she asked any questions, but when he returned, she had a what-are-we-doing-here look in her eyes.

He turned down the radio. "Since Mustang Valley doesn't have a gun range, I though we might do some shooting out here."

"Whose property is this?" she asked, taking in the crooked fence posts, the sagging barbwire and the shed on the north quarter of the parcel.

"Mine."

She looked around curiously at the flat, empty acres that had once held cattle but now stood empty. "You planning on doing some ranching?"

He snorted. "I don't fancy going broke, but my father had big dreams. This place is the only thing he left me and it's pretty worthless. But I pay the county fifty dollars a year in taxes to keep it, anyway."

"You never talk about your family." He heard the toned-down interest in her voice.

"Not much to say. Didn't know my mother. She ran off and never looked back. Dad drank himself into the grave."

He caught the pity in her blue eyes before she stared at the horizon. But she kept her tone casual. "You don't any have cousins, aunts, uncles? No one?"

"You don't miss what you've never had." The last thing he wanted was her sympathy or to speak of the aunt and uncle who'd raised him. He threw the Jag into gear and eased over the bumpy, overgrown pasture.

She seemed to realize he didn't want to pursue the

subject. He didn't mind when she tipped back her head on the seat and closed her eyes. A soft little smile played across her mouth, and he would have given tonight's take at the bar to have known her thoughts right then.

He headed for the shed his father had built almost four decades ago. The structure needed a paint job, but last summer Wade had reshingled the roof. The timbers were sturdy and the chained doors kept out vandals—not that there was all that much inside worth stealing—just a few guns and ammunition, a worn-out saddle and bridle and crates of assorted junk that he'd never thrown away.

"So you're going to give me shooting lessons?" That mysterious grin was back on her lips. He wondered exactly what had so amused her.

"I hope you never have to use the weapon your father gave you, but you should know how."

"Okay."

At least she didn't seem to mind that he'd taken a detour from their investigation. He stopped the car by the shed, opened the combination lock and pulled back the doors. Kelly peered inside, her eyes alight with interest, her golden hair gleaming in the sunlight. If she'd been any other woman he would have considered taking out the blanket he kept in a storage trunk, spreading it over a thick patch of grass and...

*Don't go there.*

She's Andrew's sister. Untouchable.

"Why don't you take your gun out of the glove compartment?" he suggested, not liking the way the gentle breeze carried her scent to him. A light floral scent that reminded him of orange blossoms and rain-kissed flesh. Reminded him of a hot summer night when he and Andrew and Kelly had seen a movie and shared a bucket of popcorn. Her lips had been the same color of pink that night as they were this afternoon, and just as unkissable, he reminded himself.

While he gathered milk crates, empty milk jugs and set up targets, she returned to the car, retrieved her gun and rejoined him. She held the weapon pointing downward between her thumb and pointer finger, her nose squinched up as if she were holding a dead skunk.

He restrained a laugh. Apparently, not even the ridiculous pink holster could make the weapon an acceptable accessory. She was right in one respect. Kelly was all lean, soft curves and feminine delights. The hard metal gun in her hands was almost jarring.

He took the weapon from her fingers, surprised at the weight. "This gun is no Saturday night special."

"Really?"

"It's a 9 mm semi-automatic Beretta." He should have known that while Mr. McGovern didn't know enough not to give his daughter a gun without instructing her how to use it, he wouldn't buy anything cheap, either. Only the best would do when it came to Kelly McGovern.

Wade didn't blame her father. The woman had aroused Wade's protective instincts, too. And he wouldn't allow her to shoot herself in the foot because he hadn't bothered to teach her how to use the weapon.

"So it's a good gun?" Kelly asked.

"Yeah." He took the gun away from her so she

wouldn't drop it in the dirt and get sand in the clip. "I have plenty of ammo."

She shuddered. "You mean we're going to shoot it more than once?"

"Why don't you like guns?"

Kelly looked up at the sky and rolled her eyes. "Who said I didn't like them?"

He checked the safety, which was on, then slipped out a fully loaded clip which slid smoothly into his hand. The gun seemed well oiled and good to go. He checked the chamber. Empty.

He turned his attention to her. "Let's get you outfitted."

She smoothed her blouse, tightening the material over her breasts. "I don't like the shoulder holster. I tried it on for Halloween once, since I thought it would go with my Annie Oakley costume I had made in a special pink leather to match the holster, but the weight made me lopsided, creased my blouse and was just danged uncomfy."

He pictured her as Annie Oakley in a Stetson hat, a short pink leather skirt and vest with matching fringed boots and restrained another grin. "I meant we need to wear protective gear."

"Protective gear?" She frowned at him. "Are you afraid I might shoot you?"

He chuckled. For a smart woman she could be amazingly dense. He handed her a set of sound-deadening ear protectors. "Here you go."

She took the ear guards from him as reluctantly as if he'd handed her a live snake. "That's going to mess up my hair."

"You really don't want to shoot this gun, do

you?'' He wondered if she was thinking about Andrew's being shot, but he couldn't afford to let her out of this, not with their lives at risk.

"I could think of better things to do." Her voice purred like a kitten's.

Better things? Like making love on that old blanket of his in an empty field?

His mouth went dry. Although he couldn't decide if her word choice had been deliberately flirtatious, he knew ignoring it would be best. Taking a moment to calm his galloping pulse, he threaded his fingers through his hair.

"Look. Someone may be trying to kill us, but even if they aren't, it's dangerous to carry a loaded gun when you don't know how to use it."

"Okay." She placed the protectors over her ears. "You don't need to be mean about it."

Mean? Had his irritation at the images she brought to life in his mind caused his voice to turn harsh?

He handed her the gun. "First thing you need to know is that even if the gun's unloaded, never point it at anyone unless you intend to shoot them. Treat the weapon as if it's always loaded."

"Got it."

"Here's the safety. When it's in this position, you can't pull the trigger."

"Got it."

"All right. Here's the clip. Ram it home."

It took her three tries but she finally loaded the gun, almost dropping it twice in the process. But at least she never aimed it at him.

"Take off the safety," he instructed.

She fumbled around but finally flicked the switch. "Now what?"

"Aim at that milk jug, but don't pull the trigger."

"Okay." She poked the gun in the direction of the milk jug, reminding him of a fencer trying to jab an opponent.

"You're going to shoot the gun, not stab someone with it."

She arched her brow and shot him a sarcastic glower. "Now, how did I miss that?"

Ignoring her fit of pique, he issued instructions. "Look through the sight."

She lifted the gun but it drooped. "It's heavy."

"Use two hands."

"Show me," she demanded, and handed him the gun.

"Like this." He braced the wrist of the hand holding the gun with his other hand and looked down the barrel.

She tried but her hands were positioned all wrong.

"Wait a sec." He took her hand and placed it over the other. Her flesh was warm and soft, her pulse racing.

"All right, now, pull the trigger."

She closed her eyes and jerked the trigger. The gun fired and she fell back flat on her butt and almost dropped the gun. Furious, she yanked off the ear protectors, stood and rubbed her butt. "You didn't tell me it would kick me on my—"

He sighed and bit the inside of his cheek to keep from laughing out loud. He knew damn well that a 9 mm didn't have that much kick but played along with her theatrics. "Sorry."

She glared at him like a hissing kitty cat after a bath. "I'm going to be sore. And I now have a grass spot on my jeans."

"You'll live. Put the ear guards back on and try again. This time I'll hold you."

"Fine." Haughtily she put the ear protection back on. "But if you let me fall again, this lesson is over."

He stood behind her and she leaned against him, her hair brushing his cheek, her scent wrapping around him in a sensual cocoon. And that's when he realized he was in trouble. The stance was too intimate, their bodies way too close. With her back to his chest, her bottom nestled against his front and her hips nestled to his crotch, he couldn't ignore the heat seeping into him. Couldn't prevent his reaction to her wriggling to mimic the stance he'd shown her as his arousal tightened the seam of his jeans.

When the gun sagged in her hands, he clenched his teeth in frustration at their enforced proximity but reached around her to help hold the gun. His cheek brushed hers. Her hair tickled his ear. And her scent drove his pulse crazy. "This time, don't close your eyes."

"Why not?"

"Well for one thing, you'll be able to see if you hit your target." His voice came out huskier than he would have liked and he could no longer tell if his hands were steady.

"How will I know if I'm on target?" she demanded, and he realized she was playing word games with him again. He didn't know if he wanted to turn her around and kiss her or turn and walk away.

"You'll know," he assured her.

"Now what?"

"Pull the trigger."

"Okay."

She shot. And shot and shot, the gun wildly raking the grass or firing harmlessly into the air but never once hitting the milk jug. And when the bullets ran out, she flung herself around in his arms, a pleased grin on her face. "I did it. I did it."

Her laughter was contagious but he shook his head. "You didn't hit anything."

"Not yet." And that's when she planted a kiss on his lips and hugged him so tightly that she cut off his breath. Or perhaps it was his tripping heart that cut off his oxygen circulation, but he suspected it was likely her mouth pressed to his, her breasts flattened against his chest, her hips molded to his. With her arms around his neck, one hand in his hair, her mouth encouraged him to kiss her back with tantalizing boldness, and he did what came naturally. He obeyed what hundreds of thousands of years of male instincts told him to do. He gathered her close and kissed her back.

Hot damn, the woman could kiss. And fire him up hotter than a rodeo cowboy on Saturday night. She teased, she taunted, she nipped and she yielded her soft body to him so that he had difficulty knowing who was taking and who was giving. His thoughts spun, and a heady feeling of happiness swept over him. Holding her in his arms was pure pleasure. She was wonderfully soft, fantastically erotic and so…not…for…him.

Gasping for air, he pulled back and scowled at her. "Just what the hell were you thinking?"

"I was thinking that one kiss isn't nearly enough."

He didn't like the way he'd responded to her, as if hit with a lightning bolt of passion, and he hardened his tone. "One kiss—was one too many. I didn't bring you here to fool around."

She glared at him. "Well I don't know about you, but I certainly hit *my* target."

"This is serious."

She tucked the gun into the waistband of her jeans. "When have I ever indicated that I wasn't serious?"

"I was talking about you learning to use the gun."

"Oh, for heaven's sake. Hand me some ammo."

She removed the clip in one smooth motion. He gave her bullets and she loaded the clip with no instruction, without fumbling once. She rammed the clip home like an expert. Then she placed the ear protectors over her head, spun around and fired. The plastic jug jumped and while it was in the air, she hit it again. And again.

He'd been had.

"I thought you said that your father never taught you to use a gun?"

"He didn't. Andrew did."

"And you let me think…"

"Whatever you wanted."

All her pretending had been to get him to put his

arms around her. Anger and admiration and lust battled within him, and when she turned around he raised his hands in mock surrender. "Okay. Okay. You win."

## Chapter Eight

"What do I win?" Kelly asked, allowing her happiness to show in her eyes.

Wade's kiss had been fantastic. With all the excitement sparking through her, and her lips aching for another kiss, she had a little difficulty following the conversation. But somehow she didn't think words mattered so much right now. Not with that heat in Wade's eyes that fired a piercing shot to her heart.

Man, oh, man, he was yummy. He kissed like a dream, his eyes turned to smoke and he looked like some kind of dangerous angel who would like to ravish her in one gulp. And still he held back. Maybe he still felt guilty for living instead of dying like Andrew, the way she had at first. Sometimes her feelings for Wade made her feel selfish. But she just couldn't think about Andrew or finding his murderer all the time. His death was still too painful and there was nothing wrong with her and Wade exploring their growing friendship—one that she believed Andrew would have eventually approved of. She had no idea from where Wade summoned so much fierce self-control because she could see the desire in his eyes, feel the need radiating off him in waves, hear the rasp in his words.

His nostrils flared and the pulse in his neck thudded erratically. ''You win the best-kisser-of-all-time award.''

''And?'' she prodded, holding herself stiffly, somehow already knowing he intended to reject her again. Although disappointment washed through her that he wouldn't be reaching to take her back into his arms for another extended kiss, she took heart in the fact that each time he denied her he had more difficulty doing so. She inhaled through her nose, let the breath out slowly through her mouth and braced her feet to steady herself against whatever he said next.

''And it's time to call Johnny again,'' he reminded her.

Damn him. He just had to go and throw their investigation into her brother's murder in her face. She swatted down the guilt that she was messing around with Andrew's best buddy, while her brother rested in his grave. Andrew would want her to live. She would allow herself to miss her brother, but she would not regret kissing Wade—not ever.

Besides, if Wade was feeling half of what she was, he wouldn't be able to resist her much longer. Their growing friendship and trust in one another wasn't just one-sided. She liked him a lot. She admired his loyalty to her brother and his work ethic, and did as Wade suggested and took out her cell phone again. While she called, Wade collected and stored the crates and empty milk jugs and extra ammunition.

"Johnny still isn't answering," she told him.

"Well, we have two choices." Wade relocked the shed, his strong fingers snicking the chain tight. He moved with such smooth confidence, she wondered what those fingers would feel like on her skin, and flushed at the thought. Wade paid no attention to her, testing the lock. "We can head into Dallas to talk to Debbie West's ex-husband or we can drive back to town and hope Johnny shows up."

"It's kind of late in the day to drive into Dallas. Besides, I'd rather try and line up an appointment with Niles. A businessman like him is bound to be busy, and for all we know he could be out of town."

"All right. We head back to Mustang Valley," Wade agreed, allowing her to make the choice.

She liked the fact that Wade often let her make the decisions. Other men—and their egos—felt threatened by her. She'd never been around anyone as strong or self-sufficient as Wade, or anyone who seemed to have as little to prove. His self-confidence allowed him to treat her as an equal and she liked the way he made her feel valued and special. Wanted.

Oh, he might be temporarily resisting, but he wanted her all right. During their kiss, she'd felt his arousal pressed against her. But she didn't understand his reason for playing hard to get. She wondered if he'd made some kind of promise to her brother to hold back, or perhaps it was more simple. Perhaps he just hadn't had a woman in a long time and, while he was aroused by her, he didn't like her enough to pursue her.

She didn't like that possibility.

However, Wade could be remarkably close-mouthed when he didn't want to talk. He'd mentioned his family, giving her a brief explanation that was civil, without going into details. Coaxing him to talk about his reasons for rebuffing her wouldn't be easy—yet that didn't deter her one whit. Although she understood that part of his resistance was because she was Andrew's sister, she didn't know his exact reasons. Wade was a man worth putting forth some effort to understand. And she planned to do much more than understand him.

"What are you thinking?" Wade asked on the drive back into town.

"Why do you ask?" she countered.

"You have this mysterious smile on your lips. One corner of your mouth is turned up as if you have a delicious secret and are about to burst into laughter."

"Really? I'll have to be more careful," she told him, seemingly not at all disturbed by his observation. In fact his watching her so closely and asking that kind of question revealed that her tactics this afternoon were working on him on several different levels. And she saw absolutely nothing wrong with thinking about their relationship as they searched for Andrew's murderer. Thinking about Andrew all the time was just so sad that she had to allow herself a respite. And it wasn't as if they weren't already doing everything in their power to figure out what had happened.

"So what were you thinking about?" he repeated.

"You don't want to know." She deliberately evaded the question and challenged him to provoke his curiosity.

He pulled out onto the highway. "I wouldn't have asked if I didn't want to know."

"Okay. I was thinking about you."

"Could you be more specific?"

"I was thinking about how you reacted to our kiss."

He glared at her.

She grinned. "I told you that you didn't want to know. Despite all Southern-belle rumors to the contrary, women do think about sex, you know."

"Did anyone ever tell you that you're incorrigible?"

She sighed. "Maybe that's why I can't seem to keep a boyfriend."

"That's not what I heard. Andrew told me you've left a trail of broken hearts all over Texas."

"Andrew loved to exaggerate. But he also understood women."

He shot her a sideways glance. "Meaning I don't?"

"You don't understand me."

"Well, we can agree there."

"Damn it." Her frustration level rose several degrees until she felt hot enough to turn the air conditioner down to its lowest setting. "Why must you do that?"

"Do what?"

"Agree with me."

"You want me to argue?"

"You agree with me when you want me to shut up."

"Well, it beats the alternative, which would be kissing you."

Now that was insulting. "And kissing me is so terrible because…?"

He chuckled, and she realized too late he'd been teasing her. However, she still wished he'd answer her question. But he let her words hang in the air between them unanswered.

Instead of satisfying her burning curiosity, he kept his eyes peeled on the road and was clearly maintaining his focus on why he was with her. "Why don't you try calling Johnny again?"

JOHNNY STILL HADN'T ANSWERED his phone, so they drove by the mayor's campaign office again. No one there had seen or heard from him all day. Kelly was about to call it quits. After spending the afternoon with Wade, she was both tired and encouraged. She looked forward to a peaceful dinner and evening at his place to wear down his resistance to her a little more. Maybe, if she got lucky—a lot more.

Too bad it wasn't politically correct to use Shotgun Sally's tactic. Kelly had no doubt her ancestor might have just pointed her gun at her man and made him admit that he wanted her. However much that idea appealed to Kelly, she figured that going to such extremes wouldn't be necessary, not after that wondrous kiss that had curled her toes and lightened her heart. Not after Wade had seemed just as stunned as she'd been at the embers they'd kindled and sparked into flames.

Whew. Just thinking about that kiss gave her an edge. Because no matter how cool and disinterested Wade acted, she knew better. Chemistry, lust, attraction, whatever she wanted to call the electric tension between them was there, all right. What she didn't know was if he had any feelings for her.

One thing at a time.

"Let's drive over to Johnny's apartment." Wade clearly had his mind on their search for her brother's "friend." Wade drove from the mayor's campaign headquarters toward a residential section of town. The quiet streets and homes with green lawns along with kids playing tag or riding their bikes seemed to mock the idea that Johnny might be in town for nefarious purposes.

His quadplex was a neat brick one-story where he rented one of the four units in the building. Wade parked the car and they both strode down a brick sidewalk to the front door. She didn't see any interior lights shining through the windows. Nor did she hear a TV or stereo, either.

Kelly's nerves were on edge. Of all the suspects on their list, in her opinion, Johnny was one of the most likely to have killed her brother. His motive of revenge, for retaliation at Andrew's getting him kicked out of law school by reporting him for cheating, seemed a simple reason for hatred. And when all his friends had graduated and gone on to practice law and Johnny had been unemployed, had his anger at her brother erupted into violence? She didn't know, but as Wade knocked on the door, Kelly was very glad to have him by her side.

When no one answered, Wade knocked harder.

Johnny's door remained closed, but the neighbor opened his. A thin man in his early twenties peered at them through thick glasses. He held a baby in his arms and a toddler sat on his foot, her tiny legs wrapped around his ankle.

Wade spoke apologetically. "Sorry to disturb you."

"No problem," the neighbor replied. "The walls are so thin we tend to hear everything. That's why Johnny's such a great neighbor. He's a quiet one."

Kelly couldn't help recalling all the interviews she'd seen on television after a murder where the neighbors claimed the shooter had always been quiet. She shuddered a little.

Observant as always, Wade placed an arm over her shoulder. "You wouldn't know where we could find Johnny would you?"

"Go, Daddy. Go," the toddler demanded, obviously disappointed her ride had ended.

"In a minute, honey pie." The man popped the baby's pacifier back into its mouth and spoke to Wade. "I have no idea where he went, but you're the second person who's asked me about him today."

Kelly covered her surprise and kept her tone casual. "Who else asked?"

"The sheriff came by around three o'clock. I told him the same thing I'm telling you. I haven't seen Johnny all day. I'm afraid I'm not much help."

"Thanks, anyway," Wade said and turned as if to go.

"You said you had no idea where Johnny went."

Kelly took a stab in the dark. "What makes you think he was going somewhere?"

"When I went out to pick up my newspaper, I saw him place an overnight bag in his car trunk. I might have stopped for a conversation, but the baby started crying, so I just waved and headed inside."

"Okay. Thanks again." Wade handed the man one of his business cards. "If he shows up, would you ask him to call me?"

"Sure." The neighbor shut the door, and Wade started to steer Kelly back to the car.

They'd reached a dead end. Kelly wondered what Cara would do if she were on a story. Cara never gave up, which was what made her such a good reporter. Her friend would knock on doors, pester every neighbor.

"Maybe we should question the other people in the building," she suggested.

"Good idea." Wade hugged her a little tighter. "It was also great that you picked up on Johnny having gone somewhere. I didn't catch that."

"Thanks." Wade didn't mind that she'd thought of something that he hadn't. In fact, he seemed pleased by her initiative. Kelly had never realized before how often she'd hid her intelligence when she'd been with other men. She'd learned early in life that men liked to believe they were smarter, and she'd let them, but in doing so she'd suppressed a part of herself that she missed. Using her brain was satisfying, and she appreciated being with Wade because he had enough confidence in himself not to be threatened by her intelligence.

She complimented him in turn. "I'm not sure I'd

have had the courage to knock on his door if you weren't here with me," she admitted. "And now that Johnny's left town, he seems even more suspicious."

"He could be perfectly innocent. Maybe he had a hot date or went to Fort Worth for a job interview."

That was another thing she liked about Wade. He could disagree with her, presenting another possibility without putting down her or her idea. He simply mentioned another side of things and he didn't seem to care who was right—as long as they solved the mystery.

They strode around to the other side of the building, and Kelly rang the doorbell. A white-haired lady cracked open the door and peered at them. "I'm not buying anything."

Kelly chuckled. "We aren't selling anything, ma'am. We were hoping you might know where your neighbor Johnny Dixon has gone."

"Never heard of him." The neighbor slammed the door.

"Okay." So much for Kelly's polite demeanor making friends and influencing people's help, but she wasn't about to give up. "Let's try this last apartment."

Wade knocked, but there was no answer. "Looks like we struck out."

Disappointed, Kelly headed back along the sidewalk to where Wade had parked the car. "We can try again tomorrow."

But she halted as an old souped-up Mustang pulled into the space opposite the apartment door they'd just tried. A man got out of the car from the driver's side, a woman from the passenger side. With her short, curly blond hair, petite figure and snappy dress style, she would have been pretty without the frown marring her face. The man scowled first at the woman, then at Wade and Kelly who were blocking his path.

There was a tension about the couple that suggested they'd been arguing. The woman had drawn her red lips into a pout, and her eyes brimmed with tears that had yet to escape down her cheeks. The man's body language, his too-stiff shoulders and ramrod straight spine, plus the set of his tense neck told Kelly that she and Wade could have picked a better time to ask their questions. But they were there. The couple probably didn't even know Johnny—after all he had just moved to town several weeks ago.

"Excuse me, sir." Kelly shot the man her best friendly grin. "I'm looking for Johnny Dixon."

"You and every other slut in this town," the man sneered.

Beside her Wade bristled. Kelly took his hand and squeezed his fingers, signaling him to stand down. She wanted information not a fight, and let the insult slide. "You mean Johnny has someone besides..."

"Yeah. You'll have to get in line behind my *wife*." The man barreled around them and went inside. Apparently his wife knew Johnny better than her husband liked.

The woman stared after her husband, clearly reluctant to follow him inside. Kelly strolled over to her, and the woman lifted her chin. "Don't mind Kevin. He's jealous of every man I talk to."

"So you've spoken to Johnny? Do you know where we can find him?" Kelly clued in on the hesitation in the woman's eyes. "Please, it's important."

"He left this morning."

"Did he say where he was going?" Wade asked.

"Yeah. He said he was heading to Fort Worth and that if he returned it might be to pack and leave for good." The woman sighed. "It's probably just as well. Kevin, my husband, and Johnny might have got into a shooting match if he had stayed—but there was nothing going on between us. I swear it."

"Johnny had a gun?" Wade asked.

"Yeah. It was the only thing he and Kevin had in common."

WADE THOUGHT HARD while Kelly thanked the neighbor. He took her hand and pretended to head toward the car until the neighbor disappeared behind his front door. "Why don't you wait in the car?"

She peered at him with suspicion. "You trying to get rid of me?"

For once he cursed her sharp intelligence that let her see right through him. But he didn't bother to lie and hoped she wouldn't give him an argument over his plan. They needed more clues, and right now he saw only one way to obtain them.

He kept his voice low. "Unless you're up for breaking and entering, I suggest you do as I asked."

Her blue eyes narrowed but not before he saw a glimmer of excitement mix with blatant disapproval. "You're going to break into Johnny's apartment? How?"

"That lock is so flimsy, it wouldn't keep out those stone-throwing juvenile delinquents."

Wade extracted an army knife from his back pocket and opened a thin blade. He picked the lock as easily as if he'd used a key. Striding inside, he perused the living area. The overstuffed chair and threadbare couch probably came with the place. The tiny kitchen that extended off the living area had a peeling linoleum floor but was spotless—probably never used.

"If you're coming inside, hurry up before someone sees you," he instructed.

Kelly stepped over the threshold and shut the door, but just stood there as if she couldn't believe she'd actually accompanied him. "What are we looking for?"

"Anything connected to Andrew. Anything that might tell us where Johnny went. And I'd like a look at his gun—that is, if he didn't take it with him." Wade headed into the bedroom to search, figuring that was the likeliest place to stash a weapon.

Johnny's clothes hung in the closet. He still had socks and underwear in a battered bureau. A stack of law books sat piled on a rickety nightstand. Obviously, Johnny intended to return and pick up his things.

Wade searched under the mattress, in the closet and bureau but he found no sign of a gun. He found no notes in the nightstand. No diary. Nothing to go on.

A quick search in the bathroom revealed a bottle of aspirin, a half-used bottle of shampoo. No razor.

No toothbrush. The man expected to be gone at least overnight, just as the neighbor had claimed.

"Wade."

"Yeah?" He left the bedroom and joined Kelly in the living room.

She pointed to an answering machine. "I played back his messages. There's one from the sheriff, two from campaign headquarters asking his whereabouts. Now listen to this." Kelly pressed a button.

And Wade heard a familiar voice that he couldn't quite identify until the speaker gave them her name. "Johnny. This is Lindsey Wellington at Lambert & Church. Call me back immediately. It's important."

Kelly peered at the machine. "She left that message last night. I think Johnny got the news and forgot to erase it." She looked at Wade. "Did you find the gun?"

"No."

"Neither did I. Maybe he took it with him. Or maybe he keeps it in his car like I do." Kelly looked around, her eyes bleak. "Can we get out of here?"

Wade checked his watch. "If we hurry we might catch Lindsey at Lambert & Church before she goes home for the day. I'd like to know why she called Johnny and what was so important."

When Kelly and Wade caught up with the attorney, Lindsey Wellington didn't look as if she would be heading home for several hours. The last time they'd been in her office, her desk had been immaculate, but now notes covered the surface. She'd taped a plat map to the wall. Obviously she was busy, yet she greeted them with a friendly smile.

"Wade. Kelly. I'm just going over the paperwork

for the Wests' sale of their property. It was Andrew's deal, but I know he was concerned over the details. I figure it's the least I can do for the fiancée and her family. Please. Come in. Have a seat. What can I do for you?''

Kelly took a chair. ''Thanks. Andrew would have appreciated your help, I'm sure.''

Wade could see that Lindsey was busy and got right to the point. ''We're looking for Johnny Dixon. Do you have any idea where he might be?''

''As a matter of fact, I might. Johnny's work on the mayor's campaign was only temporary. Andrew had hoped to find him a permanent job at city hall but it didn't pan out. I happened to speak with a friend of mine in Fort Worth, and she mentioned that her firm was looking for a law clerk and I suggested Johnny.''

''Would you have the address of the law firm?'' Wade asked.

''You're going all the way to Fort Worth to find him?'' Lindsey's Boston accent thickened. ''What's so important that you can't wait until he comes back?''

Wade exchanged a long look with Kelly. He would leave it up to her to decide whether or not to tell Lindsey that Andrew had been murdered. And that one of their prime suspects was Johnny Dixon.

Kelly didn't answer Lindsey but asked a question of her own. ''Can you tell me what Johnny's attitude toward Andrew was like?''

''What difference does it make now?'' Lindsey asked. She paced behind her desk, as if setting her thoughts in order. ''I only saw the two of them together twice. Once here at Lambert & Church and once at lunch at Dot's. Andrew treated Johnny like one of his lost sheep. He seemed to collect people who needed his help.''

''But what was Johnny's attitude toward Andrew?'' Kelly pressed.

''If you're asking me if he murder—''

''Who said anything about murder?'' Kelly asked.

''I heard a discussion when I was at the coffee machine.''

Kelly shrugged. ''I should have known. After all, this is Mustang Valley. Word gets around.''

Lindsey spun around and headed back in the opposite direction, her quick steps eating up the distance. ''Johnny is desperate to get a job. I had to lend him gas money to drive to Fort Worth.''

''So he won't be staying overnight in a hotel,'' Wade surmised, but then, why had he taken his toothbrush?

Lindsey stopped pacing and leaned over her desk, peering at a bunch of notes. ''Actually, the company where he's interviewing said they'd put him up for the night.''

So much for the missing toothbrush.

''It's odd that he took off without telling anyone at the mayor's campaign headquarters,'' Kelly muttered, probably recalling the messages on the machine. Wade would also like to know why the sheriff had left a message and also stopped by the apartment but he might be following up on Andrew's case.

Wade went back to a statement Lindsey had made earlier. ''So what's your opinion of Johnny?''

"Obviously, I wouldn't have recommended him if I didn't think him qualified."

"I was talking about whether he still harbored any ill will toward Andrew," Wade explained.

Lindsey folded her arms across her chest. "I'm not a mind reader."

"But you have an opinion?" Kelly pressed.

"My opinion is that under extreme pressure any person is capable of losing control of themselves."

"And was Johnny close to the edge?" Kelly prodded even harder.

"I'm a lawyer not a psychiatrist."

"We aren't in a court of law asking for expert testimony. I'd just like your opinion." Kelly walked around the desk. "Please, Lindsey. Is there anything else you can tell us?"

"All I know is that Johnny was broke and dejected about his future." She rustled through her memos and plucked out a piece of paper. "Here's where he intended to stay, the law firm where he interviewed and the name and phone number of my friend."

"Thanks." Kelly took the paper and began to walk toward the office's exit.

"Oh, there's one more thing."

"Yes?" Kelly turned, her forward progress halted.

"Please let me know if you find him. I'm a little worried," Lindsey admitted.

"Why?" Kelly asked.

"He promised to call me back after his interview and let me know what happened. I haven't heard from him."

## Chapter Nine

Kelly had mostly stopped feeling bad over enjoying Wade's company. But she still felt occasional stabs of guilt that she was alive and could talk to Wade and enjoy his friendship when Andrew couldn't. Although she was doing her best to find Andrew's killer, her brother would have wanted her to live life to the fullest, and she planned to do that.

If Johnny didn't return to Mustang Valley to work by tomorrow morning, Kelly and Wade would get up early and drive to Fort Worth. With their investigation on hold for the evening, Wade fed Kelly a bowl of his famous chili for dinner. She contributed the garlic bread and dessert, a decadent topping of melted butter and brown sugar, syrup and pecans spooned over rich vanilla ice cream. After cleaning up the kitchen, he'd checked in with his manager at the saloon, and she'd ended up on Wade's back deck in the hot tub, wondering how to get him to join her.

By now she could have supplied herself with a swimsuit, but that would have been counterproductive to her plan to seduce Wade. Except how could she begin to sweep him away when the stubborn man refused to come anywhere near her?

She tilted back her head, allowing the heat to soothe her tense muscles, but she had difficulty ignoring her nipples that pebbled every time she thought about Wade joining her. Instead, he sat several frustrating feet away on the porch swing, fully clothed, his mind clearly set against her.

Backlit by indirect lighting, he peered off in the distance—deliberately she was sure—not looking her way. His dark hair gleamed and his face appeared calm in repose, but the jut of his jaw reminded her of a man gnashing his teeth. And he kept pulling at the neck of his T-shirt as if it were too tight, letting her know that he was a lot more edgy than he was trying to appear.

What would Shotgun Sally do? Pretend to drown and then drag him into the tub with her? At the ridiculous thought, Kelly chuckled.

Or maybe Sally would pull out her gun and force him to join her naked in the tub and then let nature take its course?

She cursed under her breath.

"I heard that," Wade teased, his tone knowing, as if he could read her mind and knew exactly what was wrong. "Did Andrew know that you use language like that?"

"Andrew was my brother. My older, protective brother. And he preferred to think of me as a kid, not a woman with a mind of her own." She cupped some water and let it trickle through her fingers, enjoying the feel of the wet heat in the cool night air.

"Andrew didn't take into account that I like to be kissed and held and pursued. Hint, hint."

"I have no interest in pursuing you," he told her with a mix of both laughter and irritation.

"I suppose I should be grateful." She splashed water in his direction, sprinkling him with a few drops.

He moved his chair back another twelve inches. "Why?"

"Because after our kiss, I'd imagine that if we made love it would be...wonderful."

"You aren't making sense."

"Sure I am." She didn't bother to restrain her sarcasm. "Why would you want to feel wonderful when you can sit over there by yourself and brood?"

"I'm not brooding."

She chuckled. "If you say so. But you know shooting that gun caused me to exercise muscles today that I don't ordinarily use. I guess I'll just have to ease that soreness myself. My fingers and palms, all the way up to my forearms, require massaging." She lifted one hand out of the water and rubbed at the sore spots with the other, lingering, playing with the water, allowing the moonlight to glint off the water droplets clinging to her skin, her motions a giant caress meant strictly to entice him out of that chair.

He didn't budge. "You don't play fair," he complained, staring at her, his voice husky.

She took her time, stroking first one arm, then the other, as if she were applying suntan oil. "Too bad you won't join me because I'm sure your fingers could work out…my…aches…better than I can my-self.''

He choked on her double entendre. ''You're shameless.''

''I know what I want,'' she countered with a bold-ness that she must have inherited from her famous ancestor, because she sure as hell had never acted like this before. But she found herself enjoying the challenge of pursuing him—even if it meant throw-ing caution to the gods of lust and recklessness. She turned in the tub and folded her arms on the top ledge, then rested her chin, keeping the water up to her neck.

''You don't have a clue what I want,'' he said.

And he'd made it clear he wasn't going to tell her, which only egged her on. ''I'm not a virgin, Wade. Nor am I a tramp.''

''I've never thought that.''

''I'm choosy and I want you.'' She laid her words out with brazen abandon—after all, she had nothing to lose but her pride. And yet, even if he turned her down again, she knew every attempt was bringing her ever closer to her objective. He couldn't disguise the raw need in his tone any more than she could hold back her words. ''I suppose if you have no intention of being with me, I'll just have to take care of myself.'' At the same time she told him that, she smoothed a hand along her neck and toward her chest, stopping just above her breasts.

He groaned, no longer able to tear his gaze away from her. ''Stop it.''

''Okay.''

She stood up in the waist-high water. The moonlight glinted off her breasts and the cool night air barely lowered her internal temperature. Never in her life had she acted so boldly, but between the death of her brother and almost losing her own life the other day, she knew life could end suddenly, and she wanted to make the most of hers. She didn't want to hold back her feelings or her desire for this man, and if that took baring her body and coming to him naked, she could do so.

She'd never felt more vulnerable in her life. Or more triumphant as the hunger in his eyes reminded her of a tiger about to leap on its prey. He clenched his jaw, deepening the hollows of his cheekbones and giving his expression a savage sharpness that made her breath catch. At the sight of the bulge in his jeans, she restrained a satisfied grin.

Dipping her hands beneath the water, she cupped a handful, then splashed it over her, enjoying the wet heat and the cool air. "Come play with me, Wade."

"No."

She fisted her hands on her hips. "Why not?"

"I don't owe *you* explanations."

"You don't owe me a thing." She had no idea what made her flatten her palms on her tummy, then smooth them up her midriff until she saw him swallow hard with a fierce longing that he had no reason to deny.

He sucked in his breath and released the air in a slow hiss. "I promised Andrew that I'd look after you."

"So go ahead and look."

"Damn it. Stop playing games."

"What's wrong with playing games?" Ducking

underwater and holding her breath, she cut off any response he could possibly make. Let him stew in his own frustration. Let him wonder if she'd changed her mind. Let him—

The water churned with his arrival. He hadn't stopped to take off his clothes. In the underwater lights of the hot tub, she could see he'd kicked off his shoes, hadn't bothered to take off his shirt or jeans or socks, revealing his impatience. He seized her shoulders with his large hands and jerked her to the surface, and for a moment she considered whether she'd pushed him too far.

Then his mouth crashed down on hers, taking before she offered, demanding, and divulging a need he'd failed to deny.

*About time.*

She wasn't sure she could have faced him in the morning if he'd spun and walked away. But now that he was here, holding her, kissing her, she reveled in his clean male scent. In his clever mouth and ardent hands that roved over her back and melted her insides.

Sizzling heat pounded through her veins, and she wanted to make this last. She wanted to savor her need and his. But she felt caught up in his power, as if she'd stolen a ride on a runaway train. She wrapped her arms around his neck and hung on, plastered her breasts against his chest and kissed him back until her thoughts whirled and her heart raced on a pure adrenaline rush.

The heady feeling of knowing he wanted to resist her but couldn't had her gulping for air and grabbing his shirt to pull it over his head. He laughed into her neck and let her remove his shirt, and when they finally stood flesh to flesh, her skin skimming over his hard chest, her lips and teeth exploring his jaw and neck, she wanted more.

"Hey. Slow down," he whispered.

She nipped his shoulder. "No way."

"There's no rush."

But there was. She didn't want to give him a moment to think, for fear he might change his mind. And after joining her in the water, after tasting the caramel on his breath from their luscious dessert, after holding him so close, she couldn't bear to risk him backing off.

"Wade."

"Mmm." He nuzzled a path down her neck that left a trail of blazing heat.

"I'm not sure I can stand up while you do that."

"I'm just getting started."

That's exactly what she wanted to hear. Yet, contradictorily, she needed him to hurry. She wanted to take off his clothes, but he seemed more interested in exploring the shell of her ear. And, damn it, his hands hadn't even come close to exploring her breasts. Here she was in his arms, naked, available and he seemed more interested in her neck than getting down to business.

"Wade."

Shamelessly she arched her breasts against his powerful chest, her nipples budding with hot bliss. "Touch me."

"I am touching you. You have the silkiest skin and you taste like nectar."

He ran his lips down her neck and she shivered

in anticipation. At the same she reached for his jeans and fumbled with his belt. If the water ruined the leather, she'd buy him a new one.

Just as she reached for his zipper, his mouth closed over the tip of one breast. She gasped, her fingers losing contact with the metal fastener, her mind losing focus on the task she'd set for herself. His tongue swirled and created a magic aura that wrapped around and blanketed her in a trance, where she could only stand still and ride out the pleasure.

Any reservations she might have had about encouraging him wilted. She couldn't feel this good, this needy, this desperate unless they were meant to have this moment together. A sense of certainty, of rightness, of expectation and hope let her drop her normal inhibitions with Wade in a way she'd never done before.

As he held her in one spot with hands and teeth and tongue, her legs weakened just as her pulse raced.

"Please," she murmured, unsure of what she was even asking him for. She only knew he couldn't keep her so still. She needed to move. To use her mouth on him at the same moment he tasted her.

He bit lightly, then licked away the tingling love bite before attending to her other breast, giving it identical loving. Her fingers tugged his hair, trying to urge him on. But intent on being thorough, he held her fast, his jeans out of her reach.

"You feel too good." She tried to step back, but he kept her captured with his teeth, and the tug of his lips almost had her moaning in frustration.

"There's no such thing as feeling too good," he

murmured, his lips tickling and teasing her breast while his hand ministered to her other breast until desire welled up so hot and heavy that she wanted to pound on him to stop. Only she didn't want him to stop. She wanted more. Her entire body trembled for him, but every time she moved, he nipped and kept her exactly where he demanded.

"Damn you, Wade. I need you inside me."

"Okay." He agreed, but the foolish man kept right on with his sensual assault to her breasts until her head spun and she had to grab his shoulders to keep her balance.

"We need…I need…to take off…your jeans," she told him as a bolt of pure lust shocked her from her breasts to her toes.

"Okay." With his teeth on her breast, and one hand roving over her other breast, she didn't dare move. He had her trapped on the edge of desire, and he seemed intent on keeping her there, teasing, taunting, tempting until she was ready to scream with a longing for release.

His free hand dipped between her thighs, teasing the curls, and she didn't know if she parted her legs for him or if they were already parted. She only knew she'd never felt so vulnerable, so lusty, so ready to explode. Just a few caresses of his fingers between her slick folds would drive her over the edge. She trembled with anticipation, every muscle tensing for his touch.

She waited. And waited, but he always seemed to miss the exact spot where she needed him most. And then it struck her that he was reading her like a book, keeping her right on the edge on purpose, denying her the ultimate pleasure just to drive her crazy with frustration.

"I can't take…much more."

"Okay."

To her surprise, he released her. He placed his hands on her waist and lifted her out of the tub, setting her bottom down on the deck with her legs dangling into the water. The cool breeze on her hot skin created a sizzling sensation down her spine, but when his head dipped between her legs and his tongue licked her, she let out a short scream, half panic—half pure pleasure.

And every sensation that he'd created swept her into a tumbling cascade of need. Her head tilted back, her back arched, her breasts thrust wantonly upward at the sky. His tongue on her most intimate place, his hands cradling her bottom, his fingers holding her tipped up and open.

She flattened her palms on the deck and her knees hooked over his shoulders. And then he feasted until she squirmed, until she moaned, until she floundered wildly, caught between where he so wickedly kept her and where she so desperately wanted to go.

And when she could take no more, when every cell in her body demanded release, he pulled back, climbed from the pool and swept her into his arms.

And she didn't know whether to kiss him or curse him because she felt like a wild woman, ready to attack, he'd set her to simmering, heated her until she almost boiled over, and then he'd denied her his heat just when she needed it most. He set her down in the bedroom and made her stand still while he dried her with a towel, taking his time to caress her face and neck and breasts and back and bottom with the thick terry cloth, until she snapped it out of his hands and returned the favor.

The man had a chest that could have been on a fitness magazine. A light dusting of chest hair made him sexy as hell, but it was the heat in his eyes that jolted her into returning the favor.

She might have driven him to the brink when he'd jumped into the hot tub, but he'd just done the same to her. She clung to her sanity just barely, and did her utmost to ignore the out-of-control fire he'd stoked as she dried his back and stomach.

And finally, she tugged down his zipper. Pulling off his wet jeans took more strength than she had, but not even gravity or his slender hips came to her aid. Even with the open zipper, she tugged on the wet material, tried sliding her hands inside the waist and down his buttocks to separate the clinging denim from…bare skin. Wade didn't wear underwear.

As time passed, she regained a little control over herself and now she saw an opportunity for payback. Yes, removing his wet jeans was a chore, but when she could have tugged them down an inch, she settled for less and with each sliver of hips and thighs that she revealed, she stroked, caressed and patted.

And when his jeans finally pooled at his feet, he kicked off his socks and either he tackled her or she tackled him onto the mattress—she wasn't sure which. Nor did it matter, since their actions got them where she wanted to be. On his bed. In his arms.

She'd landed on top and he grinned up at her, his smile utterly charming. "Are you going to have your way with me, woman?"

"I believe I am."

He jerked his thumb at the nightstand. "Condoms are in the top drawer."

She leaned over to open the drawer, and he took her breast back into his mouth. Fire shot through her, and all of her need came raging back. She dropped the first condom on the floor, reached for another. He reached and slipped a finger into her delicate folds, and her hands shook so badly, she couldn't open the packet.

"Would you stop that for a minute?"

"Mmm."

In frustration she used her teeth, ripped open the packet and saw that she'd torn the condom, too. "Damn it. I need another one."

"Mmm." His tongue and teeth made movement difficult. This time she took the entire box and dumped the contents on the bed. She fumbled again, but opened the damned thing. His fingers found her and she groaned.

She needed him inside her, filling her, stroking her. This time she opened the slippery packet more carefully. Unrolled it over him, not an easy task when she couldn't see exactly what she was doing. But from the frantic motion of his mouth and his fingers, he was just as eager to join with her as she was for him.

Her breath came in raw pants. But finally she positioned her hips over him, slid down his erection. And held perfectly still. "Ah, I finally have you."

"Let me introduce you to a concept." His hands clasped her hips. "It's called movement."

"I think we should wait."

"That's not going to happen." He rolled on top of her in one swift movement.

She should have protested. He'd made her wait. He'd said she could have her way with him, but he was taking over. Not that she could complain when he felt so good. And she liked the idea of him losing control, of not being able to keep to what he'd said. Of his having to have her right now.

When he began to thrust, hard and fast, she wrapped her legs around him, drew his mouth to hers. His fullness ignited the explosion and as wave after wave of pleasure washed over her, he kept moving, kept going. She gasped for air, dug her fingertips into his back and hung on as she burst again and then again. This time he was right there with her.

Minutes later, when her galloping heart slowed and her lungs stopped burning for air, she realized that he had his hands clenched in her hair and he snuggled close, yet protectively, keeping his full weight from pressing her into the mattress.

He rolled them both onto their sides. "We need to talk."

"Mmm."

"I'm serious."

"I don't want to talk." She wanted to enjoy every residual effect of their lovemaking. Her body felt heavy and sated, more relaxed than she'd ever known. And with the buzz of multiple orgasms still in her bones, the last thing she wanted was to analyze this marvelous experience.

One glance at the determination in his eyes told

her she wouldn't like what he was about to say. She placed a finger on his lips. "Shh."

"No can do." He rolled off the bed, headed to the bathroom.

She pulled the sheet over her and closed her eyes. Maybe she could fall asleep before he returned. Wade had been absolutely yummy in bed. And his actions, the care he'd taken with her body, told her much more than any conversation could about his feelings.

She might not be able to fall asleep, but she could pretend. He took a quick shower, and by the time he returned, her breathing was steady. She could feel him looking down at her, but kept her eyes closed.

He hesitated, as if deciding whether or not to join her in his bed. When the mattress dipped, she didn't allow her smile to reach her lips. And when he slipped under the covers, she snuggled against him. His arm came around her. And then she no longer had to pretend to sleep.

TOO HYPED TO SLEEP Wade listened to her breathing. He wasn't proud of himself. He'd known better than to take Kelly to bed. He should have held back. But when she'd stood up in that hot tub, the water glistening over her breasts, he'd simply been too aroused to resist.

Instinct took over. Instincts that told him he would never forget this night and that he would regret his weakness for many years to come.

And guilt played into the mixture. He'd promised Andrew to look out for his little sister. Andrew hadn't meant make wild, crazy, awesome love to her.

So he'd disappointed the trust his friend had placed in him. What was more important, he'd disappointed himself. He didn't believe in tasting caviar when one must dine regularly on cheese and bread. One didn't test drive a Ferrari when one drove a pickup truck. But now that he'd tasted the forbidden fruit, he'd have to suffer the consequences.

He deserved the sleepless nights, the comparison of knowing other women wouldn't measure up to what she'd given him. She hadn't held back. She'd kept up. And she'd tasted sweeter than any exotic dessert.

But no way would it happen again. She'd taken the edge off his lust. Now there was no more mystery between them. They'd go to Fort Worth tomorrow, find Johnny and get to the bottom of things. Perhaps they would have to go to Dallas and talk to Debbie West's husband. And even if they never figured out who murdered Andrew, Kelly would return to school after her summer break.

He wouldn't allow himself to become any more involved. And so he allowed himself to enjoy, just this once, the fragrance of her hair on his pillow, the soft silkiness of her breast against his chest, the smoothness of her legs entwined with his.

Shortly before dawn, Wade entered that twilight zone just before falling asleep when a thud brought him to full wakefulness. Had a raccoon climbed on his roof?

Had a neighbor's dog come scrounging around his trash can?

Once again wide awake, he eased out of bed and reached for the gun on his nightstand. He didn't bother to dress but padded silently from the bedroom without waking Kelly.

It was probably nothing.

Nevertheless, he didn't turn on any lights. He stepped quietly and carefully into the living area.

The front door was closed. So was the back. But he hadn't turned his security system on after they'd come inside from the back deck. Other things had been on his mind.

He peered into the kitchen. Checked the front closet.

Nothing.

He was about to engage the system and head back to bed when he heard the creak of shoe leather scuffing across the front stoop. The hair on the back of his neck raised.

If he'd been alone, he'd go outside to investigate. But he had to stay inside to protect Kelly. Because if she ever came to harm, Wade would never forgive himself.

## Chapter Ten

A soft knock on the front door followed by a feminine "Kelly, are you awake?" made Wade realize that the female outside didn't mean any harm. However, he had no intention of opening the door stark naked with a gun in his hand.

"Give me a minute to dress," he called out.

He hurried to the bedroom where Kelly remained sound asleep, her face snuggled into his pillow. He put the gun back on the nightstand, donned a fresh pair of jeans and grabbed a shirt but didn't put it on.

Then he shook Kelly's shoulder. "Wake up, Sleeping Beauty."

"Mmm." She barely stirred.

"Wake up," he said again. He shook her a little harder. When she still didn't move, he flipped on the light, appreciating the way the golden rays kissed her skin. "Wake up. You've got company."

Kelly immediately straightened, her eyes wide open. "What do you mean *I've* got company?"

He wondered if she'd been playing possum and had pretended to sleep, but why? He frowned at the only reason he could reach—that she didn't want to speak to him. How ironic that every other woman he'd dated always wanted to talk and he hadn't. Now he needed to have a relationship conversation and in all likelihood Kelly was the one avoiding it. However, now was not the time to delve into her tactics.

He snapped his jeans. "Someone at the front door is asking for you."

She glanced at his alarm clock. "It's 6:30 in the morning." Nevertheless she scrambled out of bed, not the least self-conscious about her nudity. Although he'd seen everything she'd had to offer last night, and she could offer plenty, he couldn't help but appreciate her all over again. He liked her lean lines, her toned skin and the sparkle in her eyes.

"I should have known it was someone who wanted to talk to you," he muttered to cover up his discontentment at his resolution never to make love to her again. "My friends know better than to show up before noon." He neglected to mention that he'd been worried about a dangerous intruder, especially after he saw the fear flash in her eyes.

"Something must be wrong." She yanked his shirt from his hand. "Can I borrow that? Thanks." Then she dashed out of the bedroom. Last night she'd left her clothes by the hot tub, and with nothing to replace them in his room, he supposed she might have run off in just the sheet if he hadn't lent her his shirt.

It startled him, pleasantly, that little Miss Fashion Plate had no compunction at all about revealing her body to him. There was no false modesty about her, yet she didn't show off, either. She just acted quite natural, and he'd never realized that she was so comfortable in her own skin.

With a shake of his head and a slight grin, he trailed her to the front door. If she could greet their guest wearing nothing but a T-shirt, he needn't bother with a shirt or shoes.

Kelly swung open the door. "Cara! What's happened? Are Mom and Dad—"

"They're fine."

Cara stepped inside and shut the door behind her. She took in Kelly wearing his T-shirt and him in his jeans. Another woman might have exhibited a smidgen of embarrassment, but Cara didn't even seem surprised that they'd hooked up.

"Why are you here?" Kelly asked.

Cara glared in his direction, and he suspected she didn't want to speak in front of him, but Wade had no intention of leaving. However, he could be civil. "Coffee, anyone?"

"Thanks," Cara said. "I take mine black."

"Yes, please." Kelly frowned at her friend. "Now tell me what's so important that you had to wake me up at the crack of dawn."

"A story came across my desk last night about Niles Deagen, Andrew's fiancée's ex-husband."

"We were going to try and see him either today or tomorrow."

"That might be difficult."

"He's dead?" Wade asked from the kitchen.

"No, nothing like that. He's in financial trouble."

Cara perched on a chair as if she was ready at any moment to leap to her feet. Kelly sat on the sofa, tucked her feet under her and frowned at her friend.

"I'm not following. What does this have to do with Andrew? Or me?"

"I'm getting to that."

"Today, please," Kelly demanded, and Wade realized that even when she was sarcastic and demanding, she still maintained that polite and ladylike aura that he found so compelling—especially after the way she'd let loose in bed with him last night. She was all lady in the daytime and a tigress in bed—what more could a man want?

She's not for you, he reminded himself once again.

Cara interrupted his thoughts. "Andrew defended a man named Billy Jackson, an employee of Niles Deagen's."

"And?"

"When Niles was arrested for racketeering, Billy Jackson turned state's evidence against his boss. Billy ended up dead in a Dallas Dumpster last week."

"And?"

"The bullet from the autopsy turned out to be a 9 mm."

"The same caliber that killed my brother."

"I know it's a leap because 9 mm guns are so common, but if you could get the sheriff to compare the bullets, it might prove to be the same shooter."

"Good thinking." Wade handed Cara a mug of coffee.

"Thanks."

Kelly smiled her thanks and accepted her mug. "Since Mustang Valley doesn't have a forensics lab, the bullet that killed Andrew could be sent to Dallas for their lab to make the comparison.''

"Do we know what the D.A. has on Niles?" Wade asked.

"I asked. He's not talking. There's nothing in the public records. And the D.A. just put a huge down payment on a piece of property he can't afford.''

"You think he took a payoff?" Wade asked.

Cara sipped her coffee and spoke to Kelly as if Wade wasn't there. "You should keep him. Any man who makes coffee like this…yum.''

Kelly sputtered. "Cara!''

Wade settled his hip against the far end of the sofa, amused by the byplay. He enjoyed the blush rising up Kelly's neck and then her bold I-can't-believe-you-said-that-in-front-of-him stare at Cara.

"It's about time you went after what you wanted," Cara continued, not the least intimidated by Kelly's scowl.

"So what kind of financial trouble is Niles in?" Wade asked to get Kelly off the hook.

"Right now, it's just rumors. Talk about money and sex arouses everyone's interest.''

Apparently, Cara wasn't done teasing Kelly. But Kelly had her own way of coping. She looked at her watch and spoke sweetly. "Don't you have to be at work by seven?''

"Where does the time go?" Cara slugged down a big gulp of caffeine, stood and handed Kelly her empty mug. "Hell, I'm late, but that doesn't mean I don't realize that you want me out of here.''

Kelly stood and hugged her friend. "Thanks for the info. I appreciate it.''

Like the busy reporter she was, she hurried out the door, but then she looked over her shoulder and winked at Wade. "You notice she didn't thank me for my advice."

"I'M CALLING DADDY," Kelly told Wade and picked up the phone. She gave him a chance to protest, but when he didn't, she dialed, repeated the information Cara had given her and asked her father to make the request to the sheriff to compare the bullets that had killed Andrew and his former client Billy Jackson.

The request served several purposes. One, it would free them to track down Johnny Dixon in Fort Worth and Niles Deagen in Dallas. Two, it might take the heat off of Wade and Kelly. Whoever had tried to run them off the road just might believe they'd given up on their investigation and leave them alone. Besides, if Kelly made an outright appeal to the sheriff, she might as well take out an ad in the *Mustang Gazette* to announce their suspicions. Three, the sheriff was a lot more likely to heed a request from one of the town's leading citizens than his just-graduated-college daughter.

Next she tried phoning Johnny's room at the hotel Lindsey had written down for her. No answer. She also tried his apartment. Again, no answer. But for all she knew he was sleeping in. Yawning, she stretched and the T-shirt rose up her thigh several inches. Wade pretended not to notice, but he looked away with such studied disinterest that she knew better.

As she headed to the guest room for some clothes

and to use the shower, she wondered how long she could keep avoiding the conversation he'd wanted last night. She couldn't always pretend to be sleeping or distract him with flirtation. Sooner or later he'd find a way to pin her down and talk, but she figured the longer she could put him off a serious discussion with his telling her how unsuitable they were for one another, the more time she had to work on changing his mind, especially since the more time she spent with him, the more she liked him, as a friend—not just a lover.

Sure they'd been great together in bed, but that wasn't enough. Kelly had always longed for love, for a soul mate, for someone to share her life with, and she believed Wade might just be that man if he'd only give them a real chance.

Kelly plunged under the hot water, recalling how she'd gotten to him last night in the hot tub. He most certainly hadn't intended to make love to her, but she'd won that battle of wills, and she hoped, now that he knew how good they could be together, that his attitude toward her would soften enough to let him acknowledge his feelings. He had to have them. She certainly did. She couldn't have made love to him if she hadn't believed they had a shot at a future together, and she refused to believe Wade could make love with that kind of raw sensuality, yet still maintain that level of concern over her well-being and satisfaction without having genuine emotions toward her.

He just needed a lot of coaxing. Fine. She could do that. Her father had once told her she was a natural-born flirt. In recent years she might have curtailed those tendencies, but Wade seemed to appreciate her efforts.

What if she was wrong about Wade? Suppose he couldn't return the love and the friendship she offered? Life would go on.

Would she be disappointed? Of course. She might be devastated.

It might take a long time to move on and get over this wonderful feeling inside that told her they were so right together. She loved the way he took her ideas seriously. He never patronized her. He was steady and loyal and brave.

She wanted to continue to get to know him better, much better. And whether sharing a drive or a meal or a moonlight kiss, she always enjoyed his company. If he didn't feel likewise, she had the support of her family and her friends and an inner strength that demanded she take this emotional risk or regret that she'd failed to follow her heart. Her powerful feelings toward Wade were simply too strong to leave unexplored. Now that she'd gotten to know him, now that they'd made love and she knew how terrific he could be, she couldn't walk away and pretend he meant nothing more to her than a one-night stand.

She didn't do one-nighters. She wasn't interested in a fling. She never allowed herself to make love to a man unless she believed he had long-term potential. The fact that she'd been wrong twice before, in two other relationships, didn't deter her. The right man would come along someday—that he might turn out to be Wade excited her and propelled her to take a few calculated risks.

After showering, she towel-dried her hair, pulled it back into a ponytail, leaving a few locks to curl around her face, and applied makeup. She donned a sleeveless clingy tank top, a short flirty skirt, comfy sandals and for a touch of professionalism, she grabbed a suit jacket and packed an overnight bag in case they wound up staying in Forth Worth or Dallas.

When she returned to the living room, Wade wore jeans and a denim shirt. He was talking on the phone, something about his inventory and a bar fight, and he mentioned Rudy, the kid who worked for one of his employees and who'd broken that windowpane in town.

Wade hung up the phone. "Ready?"

"Yeah."

"Apparently Rudy has something to tell me. He's outside."

The kid was sitting on Wade's front stoop, throwing pebbles at the trash can. He stood up, shoved his hands in his pockets and mumbled, "Dad found out about the damage to that broken window and told me to come see you. Thanks."

"Apology accepted," Wade said.

As gratitude went, Rudy had spoken most grudgingly but Wade let that slide. He didn't rub the kid's nose in his mistake and she liked him for it.

"I might have some information for you," Rudy said. "But I'm not sure if it's important."

"Why don't you just tell us and let us decide?" Wade suggested.

"Dad said I'm not to bother you—but you did ask."

"That's right, I did. I can pay for information," Wade told him, reaching for his wallet in his back pocket.

"I was hanging out at the mayor's campaign headquarters, waiting for the flyers to come back from the printer so I could deliver them."

"Yes?" Wade prodded.

"Mayor Daniels was talking to Sheriff Wilson about a land deal, and when they said that the Wests were almost ready to make some money, I listened real hard. Because Debbie and Andrew were engaged, I thought you'd be interested."

"I am. The Wests are selling their ranch, and Andrew was handling the lawyering for them, that's common knowledge."

Rudy's face was puzzled. "Is it common knowledge that the mayor and the sheriff are eager for the contract to go through?"

"I have no idea why they would care, except that the West family needs that money." Wade pulled out a five-dollar bill. "Is that all?"

"Except for when they saw me, they stopped talking." Rudy shrugged. "I got the feeling I wasn't supposed to have heard what I heard."

Wade handed the kid the money. "Thanks."

"Was that important?" Rudy asked, his eyes curious as he tucked the money into his front pocket.

"I don't know. We're working on a puzzle, and you just brought us another piece. Until we have more, we can't put the clues together, so we need you to keep listening."

"Okay."

"And, Rudy…"

"Yeah?"

"Keep a low profile. That means don't get caught listening."

"Sure." Rudy strode away whistling and Wade watched him go, a lopsided grin on his face.

Kelly kept her voice down so the kid wouldn't hear him. "If you want to give him money, why don't you give him a real job, like mowing your grass or washing dishes?"

"He's not ready for hard labor."

Kelly shrugged. "It's your money."

"You don't understand."

"So explain it to me."

"On your side of town it's acceptable for kids to take a low-level, low-paying job to earn gas money. Rudy's never going to have a car. His family is too poor."

"But a steady job would earn him the money to—"

"He doesn't see it that way. He thinks working for me in the saloon would be selling out. He's afraid if he takes a job washing dishes then he'll end up like his father."

Kelly realized that Rudy reminded Wade of himself. He could have been that kid. He understood him. Coming from her upper-middle-class world with its work-hard-and-you'll-succeed ethics, she had difficulty following the logic of his statement. Or maybe it wasn't logic so much as a different attitude toward life. Could the way she and Wade looked at the world prevent their relationship from deepening?

With her optimistic nature, she expected good

things to happen, and they usually did. Wade came from a background rooted in poverty, and it affected the way he dealt with the police: suspiciously. The way he looked at life: as one giant roll of the dice. The way he dealt with her: sending mixed signals.

She had no idea what to do about it. Her parents came from similar backgrounds. They had attended the same schools, socialized with the same crowd, attended the same church.

Kelly came from a two-parent upper-middle-class household. Wade had never known his mother, and his father hadn't been there for him. She understood that how she'd grown up had helped shape her into the person she was today. Maybe that's why she admired Wade. He'd had a rough life and he'd made his own way. Successfully.

He wore his self-confidence as comfortably as his broken-in jeans. Yet he didn't come off as someone with something to prove, either. She'd really liked the way she could be herself with him, too. And after last night, she thought they could have a future together—if he'd just give them a chance.

THE FORT WORTH area was congested compared to Mustang Valley. Traffic was stop-and-go, and Wade drove. During the drive, Kelly had received two phone calls. The first had been from her father to check on her as well as to tell her that the sheriff had agreed to send the bullet that had killed Andrew to Dallas for analysis to be compared to the one that killed his client Billy Jackson. The second call had come from a worried Lindsey, who'd told them that

Johnny Dixon had never shown up for his appointment as a legal clerk.

Kelly put her phone back in her purse. "Lindsey didn't think he would miss his appointment unless something bad happened."

"I have to agree, especially since he had to borrow gas money to drive here." Wade turned right, drove past the hotel's valet parking and backed into a parking spot.

Kelly speared him with a curious glance. "Expecting to make a fast getaway?"

"Just being careful."

She didn't say more, but she opened the glove compartment, took out her gun and placed it inside her purse. Then she flipped the visor down and checked her makeup in the mirror. He was beginning to think of her makeup and clothing as battle armor. She subtly changed her looks depending on who they would meet, and he was just as sure she'd done that to him last night, too.

She'd certainly never looked more appealing than she had in that hot tub with the moonlight glistening off her wet skin. She'd set the bait and he'd walked right into her trap. Except, he didn't feel trapped, but fascinated, intrigued and eager to see just what she'd do next.

Only, this time he planned to be ready for her. This time he'd find the willpower to resist. Not just for Andrew's sake—but his own. Wade had to suppress his growing feelings for her with a savage ruthlessness before he got in too deep and drowned. Now that he knew how potent she could be, he would build up his resistance to her.

They entered the hotel through a side door and headed toward the elevator. "According to Lindsey, Johnny reserved room 504."

The elevator arrived with a family of four. Wade and Kelly exited first and followed the hallway signs to Johnny's room. Kelly knocked. Once. Twice.

Nothing.

She turned to him and shoved a lock of hair back from her troubled eyes. "Now what?"

Before he could answer, Kelly caught sight of the maid, and her blue eyes brightened. She headed toward a diminutive woman with dark olive skin, dark hair pulled back in a bun and creased brown eyes.

"Excuse me, I was wondering if you could help us?" Kelly spoke pleasantly.

The maid pushed her cart to the next room. "You need soap, towels, clean sheets?"

"My brother's friend asked me to come visit him. I've driven all the way here to meet him," Kelly improvised, telling mostly the truth but skirting the facts. "Last night he didn't answer the phone."

"He was here last night. He wanted an extra pillow," the maid offered.

"This morning he won't answer the door. I'm afraid something might be wrong."

"I call hotel security."

Kelly looked at Wade and began to protest. "But—"

Wade shook his head and she heeded his silent disagreement. "Security might be a good idea."

The maid used the phone, and two minutes later a uniformed guard joined them. "You think there's a problem in 504?"

"We don't know." Wade placed himself between Kelly and the door. "We expected Mr. Dixon to answer his phone or the door and he didn't show for an important job interview this morning."

"Okay." The guard knocked, and when he didn't get an answer either, he opened the hotel room door. He entered the room and did a quick search of the closet and drawers. "There's no one here. Looks like your friend checked out."

Wade didn't know what to think. Johnny had been desperate for this job. If he wasn't at the hotel, then where was he? "Thanks for your help. Sorry to have disturbed you."

Discouraged, he and Kelly returned to her Jag and she replaced her gun in the glove compartment. "As I see it we have two choices. We check the hospitals, the morgue and the police stations for Johnny or we go on to Dallas and speak with Niles."

Kelly sighed. "What do you think?"

"I vote we drive to Dallas. Johnny might show up later today in Mustang Valley."

Kelly clicked on her seat belt. "It's so strange. He left the mayor's campaign without telling anyone. He comes here and doesn't show for the interview. But the maid told us that she spoke to him last night."

"It's almost as if we're chasing a ghost," Wade muttered. "It's probably just bad luck. Maybe he got a flat tire on the way to his appointment."

"But wouldn't he have phoned his potential employer, who would have told Lindsey—who would have told us?"

Wade grinned. "You know you're scaring me. I actually understood that sentence."

"Why is understanding me scary?" she countered. "Women are simple creatures, really."

"Yeah, right."

"It's true. We just need good friends, a close family, a job we enjoy and someone to love."

"What about fashion accessories?" he teased.

"Them, too," she agreed.

Traffic snarled and he slowed the car. Up ahead he saw red and blue police lights and the intersection blocked. A traffic cop rerouted them.

"Must be an accident."

"Oh, no," Kelly gasped.

"What?"

"That looks like Johnny's car. I saw a picture of it in his living room."

# *Chapter Eleven*

"Is he dead?" Kelly dreaded the answer to her question but knew she had to ask.

Just minutes before, Wade had pulled into a parking lot and they'd walked over to a police officer on the scene. Yellow tape surrounded what proved to be Johnny Dixon's car. Several bushes in the median looked uprooted, and a telephone pole had crushed the car's front end. One officer snapped photographs, and another wrote up the incident while a third measured skid marks on the road.

The windshield in front of the driver was shattered and blood trickled down the glass. Kelly turned her gaze from the scene, her stomach roiling. If Wade hadn't avoided the tow truck pursuing them a few days ago, they might have been as unlucky as Johnny Dixon.

"I can't give out medical information, ma'am," the police officer replied from the other side of the cordoned area. "An ambulance took the driver to County General. You can check on him there."

Kelly didn't see any other vehicles, but a tow truck driver was hooking up Johnny's smashed car, and it appeared another car had been involved but had been removed from the scene. She saw no additional skid marks, no other signs that another car or truck could have caused the "accident."

She tried to phrase her question innocuously and ignore the sweat on her brow from the hot sun. "Was anyone else hurt?"

"No, ma'am."

Wade would understand that she was worried that someone might have run Johnny off the road, just as had been done to them. Yet she hesitated to sound too inquisitive since she didn't want to make explanations to the policeman. "Officer, were there any witnesses?"

The officer's eyes narrowed. "Why do you ask?"

"Just curious," Wade replied. "Did you find a gun in the car?"

"I suggest you take your curiosity elsewhere. You people need to move along and go about your own business."

"But—"

"Ma'am, I've told you all that I can."

At a momentary dead end, she and Wade returned to her Jaguar and the air-conditioning cooled her. She wasn't in the mood to talk. Seeing that wrecked car had shaken her more than she wanted to admit. The sight of the tow truck had brought back their own close escape from death just a few days before, and Kelly wondered if her parents had been right, that they should leave the state and hide out while the sheriff did his job. However, he might never solve the case, and then neither she nor Wade would be safe until they figured out the identity of Andrew's murderer.

"Can I borrow your phone?" Wade asked.

"Sure."

After she handed it over, he dialed and chose the speaker option so she could listen to his conversation. After several rings Deputy Warwick answered, "Mitchell here."

"I was wondering if you could request a look at a Dallas accident report for us," Wade phrased his question as a suggestion, but she heard the urgency beneath his mild tone.

"What accident?" Mitch asked.

Wade gave him Johnny's full name and the street address. "Any news yet on whether the bullet that killed Andrew matched the one that struck his client?"

"We should have an answer this afternoon," Mitch told him. "Mr. McGovern's applying pressure on the sheriff. Oh, and we got the fire chief's report. Your guy used an accelerant to start the fire at Lambert & Church. Gasoline."

"Thanks, Mitch."

Kelly had no idea which information was important. She intended to keep gathering pieces until she could put the puzzle together. Right now she wanted to talk to Johnny Dixon, so they drove to the hospital.

But no one there wanted to release any official information about Johnny's condition to anyone but family. While Kelly sat alone in the waiting room, hoping that Johnny would be all right, Wade sweet-talked a nurse into giving him information, which he promptly shared with Kelly.

"Johnny has a brain injury and is in a coma. He may not make it through the night, or he could remain in a vegetative state for the rest of his life."

"That's terrible."

"Or he could wake up any minute and be fine."

Stunned, Kelly tried to regroup. She'd been hoping for better news. She couldn't get Johnny's "accident" out of her mind. She had no evidence to support her theory that there had been more to it than the driver losing control of the car, and there was too much that they didn't know. Too many bad things had happened lately with people who had been connected to Andrew for this car wreck to be simple bad luck.

"The doctors are doing their best, but we can't do anything for him by staying here," Wade said. "I think we should drive over to Dallas and talk to Niles Deagen."

"Okay."

Kelly had never thought that playing private investigator wouldn't have consequences, but in the last few days she'd come to the conclusion that it could be a very dangerous profession, one she'd have no interest in doing full-time. But if she survived the next few weeks, she vowed that never again would she take her tomorrows for granted.

During this dangerous time with Wade she'd passed a milestone in her life. She'd changed in several ways, one of them being that she trusted her own instincts more than ever. And she now refused to live in a world where the approval of others influenced her decisions as much as she'd allowed in the past. If her parents didn't approve of Wade, that was their problem. She was a big girl and it was her decision whether or not to pursue a relationship with Wade. Or attend law school in the fall.

Right now her primary concern was to fight for justice for Andrew. No way was she backing down. As Wade escorted her into the hospital parking lot and back to her parked Jag, she quickened her steps. The sooner they figured out who had murdered her brother, the sooner she could move on with her life.

NILES DEAGEN WORKED in a penthouse suite of the Deagen Building, an architectural masterpiece of marble and mirrors. Built with oil money, the building had the opulence of a palace, with twice the security.

Kelly had made Wade stop in a department store and insisted they each purchase new clothing before this visit. As a result of the shopping spree, Wade now wore a three-piece dark gray suit and squeaky new black shoes. For herself, Kelly had chosen a conservative blue dress that brought out the color in her eyes. Earlier, Wade had been impatient with the shopping delay, but as he strode past other men and women dressed similarly, he now realized that the time they'd spent had been worth it.

They might be meeting Niles on his turf, but at least they were dressed as equals. On the drive into the city, they'd debated the pros and cons of calling ahead. Wade wanted to risk a surprise visit, but Kelly had insisted that a man of Deagen's stature would be guarded by secretaries and security. Without an appointment, they might not get to see Niles.

So Kelly had phoned and asked for an appointment. Surprisingly, Niles had fitted them in for a three o'clock meeting. They gave their names at the front desk, and a man in a uniform issued them temporary passes.

After riding the brass elevator to the tenth floor, striding down several hallways and receiving directions from two secretaries, they were finally ushered into Deagen's office. Floor-to-ceiling windows overlooked the city. Another wall housed framed works of art. The fourteen-foot-high ceilings gave the office an airy feel, the thick carpet portrayed wealth, while the mahogany furniture suggested old money.

In his early forties, Niles had thick black hair that was showing the first signs of gray at the temples. He wore gold-rimmed glasses and a custom suit. His piercing green eyes surveyed them with an authority that told Wade the man was accustomed to taking charge.

"Mr. Deagen. I'm Wade Lansing and this is Kelly McGovern."

Kelly shook Deagen's hand. "Thanks for seeing us on such short notice."

"No problem. Please, sit down and make yourselves at home, and call me Niles." Deagen didn't sit behind his desk. Instead he pulled up a chair on their side of the desk. "Debbie said you might be coming by."

"Debbie?" Wade asked. Niles's comment startled him. He hadn't been aware that Debbie still spoke to her ex-husband. And even if she had, how had she known that he and Kelly would come here?

"Please. Let's not play games. Andrew handled Debbie's divorce and then he was murdered. Debbie said you asked her questions and would likely want to talk to me, too. I suppose in your eyes that our love for the same woman makes me a suspect. But despite what you might think, I didn't hate your brother. As lawyers went, he treated me decently and I'm sorry for your loss, Ms. McGovern."

"Thank you."

It seemed to Wade that despite the sheriff's wish to keep his investigation under wraps, the news of Andrew's murder had leaked far beyond the confines of Mustang Valley. And from Niles's tone, either he was an extremely smooth liar or he genuinely held no ill will toward Andrew.

"Would you mind telling us where you were the night my brother died?" Kelly asked bluntly.

While Wade admired her tactic, he didn't think taking a head-on approach with a man like Niles was the best of ideas. And yet Niles didn't seem to mind at all.

"I was in Washington, D.C., that night with several senators and two congressmen. I'm sponsoring a bill to open up drilling in the Gulf of Mexico."

The oil executive might have an airtight alibi, but that didn't mean he hadn't hired a thug to do his dirty work. Wade was about to ask Niles about the rumors of his financial problems when the door to the office opened.

Kelly gasped. Niles smiled a welcome.

Wade turned around to see Debbie West entering

the room. She had no makeup on and wore clothes he considered much too young for her. Although he was no fashion expert, in her pink shirt and school-girl skirt, she looked about fifteen. She strode into the room, seemingly not the least bit surprised to see them. She walked directly to Niles and then sat in his lap.

Kelly and Wade exchanged glances.

Debbie kept her eyes downcast, her voice flat. "Niles and I are reconciling."

"I see," Kelly said, pain and anger swirling in her blue eyes at what she obviously considered a betrayal of her brother. "Did you ever love my brother or were you—"

"I loved him, but he's gone."

Kelly's eyes narrowed with accusation. "You expect me to believe that you loved my brother, yet he's only been gone less than two months and you seem to have moved on easily enough."

Debbie trembled and she refused to look at Kelly. Niles took Debbie's hands between his, and a tender look glazed his expression. "And I'm prepared to take good care of Debbie."

Wow. Wade's thoughts whirled at the multitude of possibilities. He'd never expected this turn of events. What bothered him most was that Niles didn't seem to care that Debbie had divorced him and then changed her mind after Andrew's death. It seemed to Wade that Niles's attitude was obsessive, off-kilter.

But Wade knew that what struck Kelly hard was Debbie's seeming betrayal of her brother, who had gone out of his way to help Debbie. That his fiancée could move on so easily had to hurt Kelly.

"Debbie, I wouldn't be so sure you've found a meal ticket," Kelly said with a bite of steel in her tone. "From the rumors I've been hearing about Deagen Oil, Niles has leveraged the business to the max and could lose the whole company."

"What does that mean?" Debbie asked with a wide-eyed-little-girl look that made Wade uncomfortable.

Niles patted her hair as if she were a dog on his lap, not a full-grown woman. "Nothing to worry your head over, sweetie pie."

Debbie stood up. "I know you have work to do, dear. I'll escort our guests out if that's okay with you."

The moment they exited Niles's office and shut the door behind them, Debbie dropped the little-girl demeanor. She straightened her shoulders and held her head up. "I can't imagine what you must think of me."

"I don't know what to think." Pain and distrust mixed in Kelly's tone. "How could you go back to a man like Niles after being with my brother?"

Several office workers who seemed overly interested in their conversation passed by. Debbie raised her finger to her mouth. "Shh. Not here."

She led them down the hallway and opened a door into a conference room filled with a long shiny table and upholstered high-backed chairs. "We can talk in private here."

Wade's curiosity burned, and he vowed to pay close attention to Debbie's words, especially knowing that Kelly, being upset that this woman had betrayed her brother might not be thinking clearly.

Debbie shut the door behind them and bit her bottom lip. "For what it's worth, I loved Andrew. I think…we could have been happy together but—"

"Right." Kelly's tone hardened. "You loved my brother so much that two months after his death you're back with your ex-husband? Were all those tears at his funeral just for show? Was my brother just another man that you used?"

"You don't understand." Debbie sagged against the wall. "Look, I could have stayed with Niles in his office. I didn't have to volunteer to talk to you, but I did because…"

"Because?" Kelly prodded, disdain coloring her words. She'd obviously made up her mind that this woman hadn't been good enough for her brother, and Wade tended to agree, although he was more open to hearing the extenuating circumstances.

Still, Wade's sympathy went out to Debbie. Wade had the feeling it had taken all of the woman's courage to speak up and try to explain. Debbie's hands trembled. She spoke quietly, the entire time keeping her head down, her gaze on the floor. "It's just that I'm not like you."

"What do you mean?" Kelly looked clearly bewildered. But Wade figured he had a better handle on Debbie's situation than Kelly did. The two women had grown up in the same small town under vastly different circumstances. Kelly had been born with a silver spoon in her mouth. Sure she'd worked hard in college, but that was a lot easier with Daddy paying the bills than it would have been for Debbie who'd probably never entertained the idea of attending.

"I never graduated high school, nevermind went to college like you. Don't you think I'd like to work and be self-sufficient?"

"How do I know? Maybe you just want to depend on a man for your every need."

Debbie shook her head. "I've learned that to get a decent job, I need skills or an education. I have neither. And I'm broke, too."

"What about the money from the sale of the ranch?" Kelly asked.

"Most goes to the bank, the rest we owe to the credit card companies. I need a friend to help me out. I couldn't make it alone. That's what I meant when I said I'm not like you. You're strong. You can stand alone."

"Did you see my brother for anything more than a meal ticket?"

Kelly headed toward the door.

Clearly she didn't want to listen to Debbie's excuses, but Wade understood what Debbie was trying to say better than Kelly did. Kelly hadn't had to clean the house; her folks had hired a maid. She hadn't had to work two jobs to help put food on the table or arrive at school so exhausted she couldn't keep her eyes open.

Wade started to follow Kelly out the door but paused a moment to squeeze Debbie's shoulder with compassion. He was about to try and think of something comforting to say when Kelly stopped, rooted her feet in the carpet so suddenly that he almost bumped into her. She opened her purse and dug through it.

Kelly pulled out her checkbook and her pink pen, then signed a check that she thrust at Debbie. "Here. Use this however you like."

Debbie took one look at all the zeros and shook her head. "I can't take that."

Kelly rolled her eyes. "Andrew would have wanted you to have a way to survive without turning to a man like Niles."

"I don't know what to do with that kind of money. I'm not smart like you."

"My brother didn't date dumb women." When Debbie still didn't take the check, Kelly folded it and stuffed the paper into Debbie's pocket. "The first thing you have to do is believe in yourself or no one else will."

Tears brimmed in Debbie's eyes. "I don't know how to thank you."

"You can thank me by going back to school with that money. Every woman should be able to support herself. And if you need help, you call me. I'll be there for you."

Grateful tears of apparent disbelief and relief at her good fortune spilled down Debbie's cheeks. "Thank you."

Kelly's change of heart and her generosity kept surprising Wade. After being so angry with Debbie, he hadn't known she could be so compassionate. Or so tough. But that toughness combined with a hefty check was exactly the kick in the butt Debbie might need to regain her self-respect and set her life on a new course.

Debbie opened the door. "Come with me. There's something I want to show you."

They headed down the hall to the elevators, but with other people riding down with them, they weren't free to talk. Kelly and Wade exchanged glances, but Kelly indicated that she didn't have a clue where Debbie was taking them, either. But no matter what Debbie showed them, Wade couldn't have been prouder of Kelly. At first she'd been so angry at what she'd seen as Debbie's betrayal of her brother that she couldn't understand Debbie's position, but once she had she'd offered a hefty check and more importantly her friendship.

They exited into the parking garage, and Debbie headed toward locked double doors by the stairs. "Niles always runs up the ten flights of stairs. He says it keeps him in shape. And yet if he doesn't get the closest parking space to the stairwell he complains like the dickens. However, he doesn't usually park his car in the locked storage area."

"Why are we here?" Kelly asked.

"Niles told me he drove to Fort Worth this afternoon for a business meeting about an oil lease, but then I got a phone call from his manager who claims he never showed up."

"I don't understand," Wade told her.

Debbie shrugged. "Niles has lied to me before of course, but then I saw his car."

She pulled keys from her pocket, unlocked the doors and pushed them wide open. Once inside the dark area, she led them to a dark green BMW parked by the stairwell. The car appeared normal until they stepped around to the front. The bumper was dented, the paint scratched.

"Looks like he was in an accident," Debbie said, stating the obvious.

Wade figured Kelly was wondering the same thing he was. Had Niles run Johnny off the road this morning? Or was Wade letting his imagination get the best of him?

Debbie folded her arms over her chest. "Niles asked a body shop owner to pick up the car at five o'clock. Seems to me he's eager to cover up his accident."

Wade called Deputy Warwick. Since Debbie had been so helpful, he allowed her to hear both sides of the conversation with Kelly over the speakerphone.

"Hey, Mitch. Did you get hold of Johnny Dixon's accident report?"

"Yeah. Hold on. Okay. I've got it right here."

"Does it mention anything about paint from another vehicle?"

"Dark green."

"I'm looking at a dark green BMW with a dent. The owner intends to send it to a body shop within the hour. If I give you the tag and location of the vehicle, can you have an officer impound the car?"

"Not without a way to tie the car to the accident, I can't," Mitchell said. "Who does the car belong to?"

"Niles Deagen."

"The Dallas oil man? We've got to be real careful. Everything by the book or his lawyers will tear us up in court. Right now you haven't given me enough to warrant a search.''

"Was there anyone mentioned in the report who saw Johnny's accident?'' Kelly reminded Wade that the cop on the scene hadn't been forthcoming when they'd asked that question. He could have been holding back information that Mitch would give them.

"There was an eyewitness,'' Mitchell admitted.

"Did the witness say anything about a green BMW?'' Wade asked.

Wade waited impatiently, and Debbie shifted uneasily from foot to foot. He hoped she wasn't having second thoughts about helping them. About helping herself.

"It's right here. A dark green BMW. Okay. I'll take care of it. Give me the location and I'll ask the Dallas police officer to impound the car. Then we can compare the paint on Deagen's car to Johnny Dixon's and see if we get a match.''

Wade moved on to his next question. "Did you get the bullet comparison done?''

"The bullet that killed Andrew came from a different gun from the one that killed his client. The case detective thought the client's ex-girlfriend committed the homicide. I heard she confessed about an hour ago. But don't give up. If the car paint matches, we'll bring in Deagen for questioning.''

Debbie frowned. "Deagen didn't even know Johnny. Why would he want to hurt him? It doesn't make sense.''

"We don't have any idea,'' Kelly admitted. "But without your help, we wouldn't have gotten this far. Thank you.''

"If there's anything else I can do to help, let me know," Debbie offered. She touched the pocket where the check resided. "I'm leaving town. You can get in touch with me through Lindsey Wellington."

"We appreciate it." Kelly hugged her. "And you should leave right away. Niles may be involved in something nasty."

"What will you do next?" Debbie asked.

Kelly shrugged her shoulders. "I have no idea."

However, Wade suspected from the pursing of her lips and the glint in her eyes that Kelly had much more than an idea.

What neither of them noticed as they left Niles's office building was the van following them.

## Chapter Twelve

Frustrated that they hadn't yet solved Andrew's murder, Kelly was at least pleased they were making progress. When they'd begun the investigation she hadn't had any leads. Now they had too many. And with clues to follow and more people to question, she was hopeful that she and Wade might eventually get Andrew some justice.

With their investigation going better, Kelly was looking forward to some serious alone time with Wade that evening. When they returned to his house after eating dinner on the road, she poured them both a glass of wine, turned the CD player's volume to low and curled up on the opposite end of the sofa from him, determined to change his mind.

"We need to talk."

He set down the newspaper he'd been perusing and gave her his full attention. "About?"

"Us."

"There's nothing to talk about." When he began to pick the paper back up, she moved closer to him, close enough to smell the shampoo from his shower and a hint of aftershave. She placed one hand on his shoulder and let her fingers play with the hair at his neck.

"We haven't really discussed our making love."

She planted a kiss at the base of his neck where his pulse fluttered erratically. Knowing that her touch affected him gave her the courage to pursue their discussion. Besides, she liked touching him, liked his response to her, liked the way she felt about herself when she was with him.

His hand closed over hers. "You're going to use every weapon in your arsenal to get what you want, aren't you?"

"Uh-huh." Since he held her hand still, she kissed a spot behind his ear.

"Okay. Fine." He shifted around to face her, ending physical contact, but the heat in his eyes warned her to tread with care. "What exactly do you want from me?"

His direct words confused her. First he didn't want to talk about them, then he claimed there was nothing to talk about and now he was asking her a question that was difficult to answer.

What did she want? She wanted him to admit he had feelings for her. She wanted him to tell her that he wanted to make love again. She wanted him to care about her as if she was his woman—not Andrew's sister.

Telling him her thoughts was out of the question, especially with him so guarded. She sipped her wine and eyed him over the brim of her glass, her heart skipping as if it knew exactly how important this discussion was to her future. He'd avoided talking about himself by asking a question first, one she didn't know if she wanted to answer.

She stalled. "Can you be more specific?"

"Do you want a fling with Mustang Valley's bad boy?" he challenged her. "Do you just need someone to console you while you grieve? Are you trying to use me to rebel out of your safe little world?"

He flung the questions at her with a curt aloofness that told her her answer meant more to him than he wanted to admit. So despite the pain he'd inflicted, she kept the hurt pinned down. "You sound as though you think that I'm using you."

"Aren't you?" His gray eyes darkened with fierce accusation. "You've known me all your life, but you've never exhibited any interest in me until now."

"Not true."

He arched an eyebrow in disbelief. "Yeah, right."

She held his gaze and kept her voice level. "I've had a crush on you since I was in the eighth grade and you were a senior in high school and took Cindy Jo Crocker to the prom. You wore that black suit and black shirt that knocked my socks off. I wanted to be Cindy so badly that night that I followed you and Andrew on my bike. You never even knew I was there, and when I lost sight of your car, I went home and cried my eyes out. And do you know why I cried?"

"Because you weren't old enough to buy a gown for the prom?"

"Cute." She shook her head. "I cried because I knew that good girls didn't go out with exciting guys with questionable reputations. You represented everything I couldn't have—excitement, rebellion, freedom. Or at least I couldn't have those things and keep my parents' approval, too.''

''That was your choice.''

''I know that now. Andrew was the brilliant older son, so I gave myself the role of being the polite Southern belle, of sticking to the rules, of making straight As and never, ever embarrassing the family.''

''Exactly my point. You and I should never have happened. We don't belong together.''

''But we do. Because I'm not that anxious-to-please adolescent anymore. The approval of others is no longer as important to me as my own happiness.''

''And now that little Miss Do-It-by-the-Book has come out of the closet, you need to prove you've broken out of your self-imposed box by making love to me? Well, we did it. You can now move on with your life.''

She set down the wineglass with frustration. ''Well, I'm trying to move on, but you keep resisting.''

''Excuse me?''

He hadn't expected her to agree with him, and it had thrown him. She wondered if he was ready to hear the words she wanted to say. Wondered if she was going too fast. Wondered if she was about to scare him away. But she couldn't hold back, and if he couldn't deal with her thoughts, then he wasn't the right man for her.

''Do you think I could have made love to you if I wasn't already halfway in love with you?''

He snorted. "You think you're in love with me?"

"Yes."

He stared at her so long that she had no idea what he was thinking. "Just how long do you think your love will last?"

"I don't know." If he kept up his attitude, she might not love him for more than another minute. "I've never been in love before." She wouldn't give him a guarantee. She wasn't ready to commit her life to him. Not unless he met her halfway. And he appeared far from believing her, never mind admitting his own feelings—which she assumed he had for her—but she could be wrong. She might be making a total fool of herself by declaring her love, and he was trying to let her down easy.

Well, she'd wanted this conversation, so now she had to be strong enough to listen to what he had to say. Only, he wasn't saying anything. He just kept staring at her with those smoky gray eyes that made her want to forget about talking, grab the front of his shirt and pull his head down until their lips met.

"You love me?" he asked, this time with less disbelief in his tone.

"Yes. I love you." She eyed him with hope and vexation. He just stared at her, his face stoic as if he'd had to endure some kind of silly prank. "Space to Wade. This is the time where you're supposed to chime in and say that you love me, too."

"What about your parents?"

She lifted her chin. "This is between you and me."

"What about Cara's opinion?"

"Ditto for her."

"And your law degree?"

"What does that have to do with anything?" For a man who'd just heard that she loved him, he certainly was throwing out a lot of objections for her to trip on. She might not have declared her love to any man before, but she was agile and vowed not to go down without a full-fledged battle.

"If you go to law school, you'll leave Mustang Valley."

And then she got it. She understood why he'd been holding back. Not because he didn't have feelings for her, but because he was afraid of losing her.

"My attending law school doesn't mean I'll leave you. Haven't you ever heard of phone calls and airplanes and vacation time?"

"You haven't thought this through."

She fisted her hands on her hips. "No. *You* haven't thought this through. You don't have the courage to take a chance on me. You're the one who's been holding back. I never thought that a man who could toss a mean three-hundred-pound drunk out of his saloon without breaking a sweat, a man who took on a murder investigation to ensure justice for his best friend, a man who doesn't give one whit what the townsfolk think about him would be afraid of me. But you're an emotional coward, Wade."

"What?"

"It's not your background or your reputation or education that's going to drive me away. It's your fear of loving me. And that means you aren't good enough for me."

She marched for the door, her heart heavy, her eyes brimming with anger and unshed tears. She'd laid her heart out for him to take. Instead he'd chosen to crush it. Well, she couldn't make him love her or make him say he loved her. And if he didn't make the effort, it didn't matter either way.

Hoping he might still change his mind didn't make the ache inside her hurt any less.

Damn him.

She brushed away an angry tear. She needed to find Cara. She wanted to talk with a friend she could count on to take her side.

Too full of anger to watch her step, Kelly knocked into a chair. The carton filled with Andrew's papers tumbled to the floor. Great. The last thing she wanted was to delay her departure. She didn't want to spend another minute with Wade right now. Still, she kneeled and randomly stacked the papers that she'd already gone through twice in hopes of finding a clue as to why Andrew had been worried that something might happen to him.

While she piled the papers, Wade squatted beside her. He straightened the tipped-over box. ''I need some time, Kelly.''

''Take the rest of your life,'' she muttered as she thrust papers back into a folder.

''I never thought you were serious about me, so it colored my thoughts and my judgment. I suppose I was protecting myself.''

''From what?'' She stopped fussing with the papers and clutched Andrew's jacket.

''From you,'' he admitted. ''I always considered you off-limits. And I didn't want to be your boy toy.''

''It was never like that. I'm not like that.'' She

didn't like that he thought so little of her. Didn't like that he thought she'd been using him. Didn't like that he didn't think she had genuine feelings.

"I understand. Now," he said, his eyes locked on hers. "But all of this is rather sudden. I could tell you what you want to hear but…"

"But?"

"It would be a lie."

"Great." His words hurt but she couldn't deny the honesty he conveyed.

"I don't want to hurt you." He spoke gently. "As soon as I figure out how I feel I'll let you know."

"So damn nice of you." Insulted and irritated, she straightened the pile of papers in her hands. "You'd better think fast because I don't intend to wait very long."

He held out the box to her to dump the papers. She started to toss the entire stack and frowned at the yellow paper at the bottom of the carton. "What's that?"

"What?"

She gestured with her chin. "I don't recall seeing that before." Kelly placed the papers on the counter, reached inside the box and pulled out the piece of folded yellow notepaper. "This is Andrew's handwriting."

"It must have been wedged in the bottom flaps until you dumped the box on its side."

She opened the paper and flattened it, her mouth dry, her hands shaking. "It's a list of owners in the Ranger Corporation."

"Isn't that the corporation that's purchasing the

West family's ranch?'' Wade asked, setting aside the box and leaning over her shoulder.

''Yeah.''

''Who's on the list?''

Andrew's scrawl was hard to read and she'd had more practice than he had. ''Niles Deagen. Mayor Daniels. Sheriff Wilson. My father, Paul Lambert and Donald Church, plus a list of twenty investors I don't recognize.'' She sighed and put down the paper. ''It doesn't seem important.''

Wade picked up the paper. ''But it might be.''

''How? There's nothing illegal about forming a corporation or the fact that Niles is a major contributor to the mayor's reelection.''

''Lots of voters wouldn't appreciate their mayor siding with big business.'' Wade snapped his fingers. ''Didn't Andrew have the mayor's financial statement in that box?''

''So what?''

Nevertheless she dug out the papers Wade was talking about and handed them to him. He scanned the typed and stapled pages. ''There's no mention of the mayor owning part of the Ranger Corporation in this document.''

She was catching on. ''If he failed to disclose his ownership and Andrew found out and confronted him—''

''It would most certainly hurt his upcoming election,'' Wade speculated.

''So he kills Andrew? It seems far-fetched.'' Kelly wasn't buying the motive.

Wade placed all the papers back in the box and left Andrew's note on top. ''Suppose the Ranger

Corporation invested in other land or businesses. Big money could be involved, and the mayor's influence might be needed to construct roads, change zoning, etcetera.''

"So what do we do now?" Kelly asked. "Go talk to the mayor?"

"That's what Andrew might have done."

*And look what had happened to him.* Wade's implication rocked her. She hadn't forgotten their earlier conversation or how he'd asked for more time to think about his feelings for her, either. She picked up her car keys. "Before we do anything else I want to speak to Lindsey and Cara."

CARA, LINDSEY AND KELLY met for a late-night snack at Dot's. Wade had refused to allow Kelly to drive there alone, but once she'd met up with her friends, he'd headed over to the Hit 'Em Again Saloon to check on business. Kelly had promised to call Wade when their meeting broke up, and he would come by and take her wherever she wanted to go.

In a corner booth, Cara and Lindsey had listened to Kelly bring them up-to-date while they'd all eaten their sandwiches. Currently they shared a trio of desserts.

Between sips of her diet cola and forkfuls of chocolate cake, Lindsey spoke. "You've got enough proof to nail the mayor for incorrectly filling out his financials for reelection but not enough to investigate him for murder."

"She's right," Cara agreed, breaking a cinnamon-raisin cookie into pieces. "The mayor doesn't even own a registered gun. I checked."

"Did you find anything useful on Niles Deagen?" Kelly asked, ignoring her slice of lemon pie for the moment.

Lindsey checked her notes. "He's been brought up on racketeering charges twice, but so far the charges never stick. The man can afford top-notch lawyers."

Cara brushed crumbs from the table. "There're still rumors going around that Deagen's company is on the verge of collapse. But since he holds the stock privately, I have no way to check the real situation. On another note, when will the sheriff's office finish comparing the paint on Deagen's car to Johnny's?"

Kelly sighed, feeling weary and emotionally exhausted. "It could take days or more. And Johnny's still in a coma."

Cara eyed her across the table. "You aren't giving up, are you?"

The tension in her must have been obvious to Cara, and she tried to make her tone sound less dejected. "What makes you say that?"

"You sound discouraged," Lindsey told her. "But you're doing an excellent investigative job."

"So excellent that all we've found are dead ends." Kelly shoved her hair out of her eyes, cut her pie into pieces but didn't eat. "I'm not sure what to do next."

Cara pointed her fork at her. "What's really wrong?"

"Nothing," Kelly murmured, but Cara knew her too well.

"It's Wade." Cara spoke knowingly to Lindsey. "She likes him. A lot."

"And how does he feel about you?" Lindsey asked the big question with unerring accuracy.

Kelly rubbed her chin, glad to get another take on Wade. "That's the problem. He says he doesn't know."

"That's so typical of men," Cara told her. "Sometimes they are the last to know."

"Sounds like a cop-out to me." Lindsey gazed sympathetically at Kelly.

Cara nodded her agreement. "Seems to me that you need to bait a trap."

Kelly raised a skeptical eyebrow. "To catch Wade?"

Cara signaled her a thumbs-up. "Him, too."

KELLY PHONED WADE to tell them their meeting was about over. He told her he would come by and pick her up within a few minutes. After Lindsey and Cara left Dot's, Kelly paid the check, then used the rest room. She'd promised Wade she wouldn't leave Dot's until he returned and she took her time brushing her hair, refreshing her makeup and checking her teeth for smudges of lip gloss.

She wouldn't give up on solving Andrew's murder, and she wouldn't give up on Wade. Somehow she'd find a way to make her life go in the direction she wanted. She wondered what her ancestor Shotgun Sally would have done if she'd been in her position, but didn't come up with any answers.

Kelly exited the rest room and bumped right into

Mayor Daniels. She teetered back into the wall. "Gosh, you scared me. Where did you come from?"

He reached out and steadied her. "Oops. You okay?"

"I'm fine."

"Good." He didn't release her arm, shoved a gun into her side. "Don't even think about screaming for help."

Oh, God.

Mayor Daniels had a gun on her.

Her weapon was in the glove compartment of the Jag.

Her friends had left, thinking she'd be safe in a public restaurant until Wade came back. But Mayor Daniels had chosen his window of opportunity with a precision that frightened her as much as the gun in her ribs.

Daniels tugged her out the back door, and she doubted anyone had noted her sudden departure or would miss her. People weren't usually that observant.

Daniels hustled her through the door into a back alley, the same way he must have come inside. So it was highly unlikely that anyone had seen him. When Wade arrived and began asking questions, neither Dot nor her waitress would be able to tell him anything useful.

Outside, the garbage bin smelled and the area lacked decent lighting. With Daniels's car parked out back, he clearly intended to shove her inside his waiting vehicle. If she got in, he could take her anywhere, kill her and dump her body. It might be days before anyone found her.

Her thoughts circled in a panic.

She needed to do something. But what?

The idea of overpowering the mayor seemed impossible. And if she struck out ineffectively and he injured her, that would lessen her chances of getting away if a better opportunity arose later.

She dragged her feet, stalling. Her mind racing. *Think.*

She had a cell phone in her purse, but even if she managed to secretly call 911, no one would know her location. She could try and break his grip and run, but his fingers dug into her arm with a strength that told her she wouldn't stand a chance.

Maybe she could play dumb. "What's this all about, Mayor? You already have my vote."

"Shut up."

"Hey, that's no way to talk to one of your constituents. My daddy always says—"

"Be quiet." He shook her so hard that she almost bit her tongue.

Talking hadn't worked. Escape didn't seem a likely option.

Kelly tried the next best thing. She stepped around him, flung her free hand around his neck as if she was embracing him.

She made her voice low and sexy. "Don't you think I'm a mite too young for you, Mayor?"

For the moment he stopped dragging her across the pavement. "What the hell are you talking about?"

At least he was no longer urging her toward his car. If she could just play dumb, delay him for long enough, use up enough precious seconds, Wade would search for her, maybe even look out the back door and find her in trouble.

"I'm talking about you and me, Mayor. I've always found you attractive, but I didn't know you liked me."

"You think I like you?" he sputtered.

"Of course you do," she said. "But I never worked up enough nerve to let you know. I'm so glad you've gone and made the first move." She ran her free hand up and down his arm. "I find powerful men, especially politicians, so-o-o sexy."

Had she overdone it? Would he fall for it?

Hurry up, Wade.

Daniels's fingers clenched her arm even more tightly, and he shoved her against his car. "This is a gun. I'm not fooling around."

Frustration and fear had her trying one last time to convince him that she was interested in him as a man, not as someone who had to fear anything she might know. "Ooh. I always liked Sheriff Wilson's gun. I didn't know that you had one, too."

"I told you to shut up. Do you think I'm an idiot? Do you think I don't know that you've been asking questions about me all over Texas?"

He flipped her around roughly. He banged her against the car and she grunted in pain as her knee struck the door. When he pulled her arms behind her back, she struggled, stomped on his foot.

In surprise and pain, he released her. She ran a few steps, then his hand clamped down on her shoulder. "Take one more step and I'll knock you out, right now."

"Okay."

She forced herself to hold still, trembling as he used a plastic garbage bag tie on her wrists, then he pushed her into the passenger seat of his car.

Fear like she'd never known made her weak, almost sick. Mayor Daniels must have killed Andrew and now he was going to shoot her, too. Only he couldn't do it right in the middle of town where too many people would hear the gunshots. He was going to drive her somewhere else.

She struggled against her bonds, but he'd yanked the tie so tightly her fingers were already going numb. She would have risked a scream except the lot behind Dot's that took overflow parking during the day was empty at this time of night.

*Think.*

He'd been in such a hurry to tie her up, he hadn't removed her purse, which still hung from her shoulder. But there was no time to dig into her purse for the manicure scissors that she might use to cut herself free. Once he got away, she would be at his mercy.

Daniels slid into the driver's seat and started the car. She had to do something to draw attention to her predicament. Something drastic. This might be her last chance to get attention and the help she needed.

Kelly leaned toward the door, raised her leg and kicked the center of the steering wheel. The horn blared.

Daniels cursed. He struggled with her leg and she slammed the back of her heel into his jaw, then pressed her toes forward and onto the horn again.

Daniels yanked her ankle and twisted. She screeched in pain but she kept kicking.

A fist shot in her direction and struck her temple. Pain exploded in her head and the world turned black.

## Chapter Thirteen

Kelly woke up just seconds later. Pain made her thoughts sharp. "You can't kill me and get away with it. I've told too many people my suspicions about you," she lied.

And she would keep lying—especially if it would keep her alive.

Daniels had stuck his gun into the waistband of his pants. He hadn't bothered with his seat belt. Or hers. She wriggled around in an attempt to grab her purse, which had slipped off her shoulder to the floor.

The next time he made a hard right, she slid to the floor and let out a yelp to make him believe that she hadn't changed her position on purpose. Behind her back, she felt around for her purse.

Got it.

She opened the bag just as Daniels reached over and lifted her under the arm and propped her back on the seat. Luckily she managed to keep the purse with her.

"Who have you told about me?" he asked, his glance at her more curious than concerned.

She wanted to name Cara and Lindsey, who he knew she'd just met. He would fear Cara and her reporting, Lindsey with her ties to the law. But in case Kelly didn't make it, she didn't want this monster coming after her friends.

"Wade knows. So does my father," she said, lying some more.

"They'll just think you came off with some goofy idea."

"Not after you plug a bullet in me, they won't," she countered. Meanwhile, she stuck her fingers into the tiny purse. Her wallet was on top, and she dug past her checkbook, hitting a tube of lipstick.

"I have no intention of shooting you like I did your brother."

So he *had* killed Andrew. Until this moment she hadn't known for sure. But why would he have admitted that to her unless he planned to kill her, too?

"You aren't going to shoot me?"

Her fingers clasped the manicure scissors just as he drove out of downtown Mustang Valley. But maneuvering was almost impossible with her weight pressed again her numbed wrists.

"Of course not. You're going to die in an accident. On Wade's land." Daniels sighed. "With him in prison for your death, my election campaign should go just as I planned."

"You're forgetting about my father. I told him about you when I found—"

"Found what?"

"Andrew left me his notes," she told him, trying to stall for time, hoping she could turn the tiny scissors into a cutting tool.

"And what did those notes say?"

"That you own part of a company—"

"Nothing wrong with that."

"Except you failed to declare it on your public financial statement." She hoped her combination of truth and lies might make him reconsider his actions. Her head ached where he had slammed his fist against her temple. And as she maneuvered the scissors, the plastic cut sharply into her wrists. But determinedly, she kept hacking away at her bonds. "The voters won't be happy with you when that information comes out in tomorrow's press."

"Your friend Cara is doing the story, I suppose."

"It's already written and has been put to bed."

Daniels shrugged. "Well then, I guess the *Mustang Gazette* may have a little fire tonight."

Daniels pulled onto the highway, and she glimpsed headlights in the sideview mirror. She prayed that Wade might be following, and sawed all the harder with the scissors. She stabbed herself repeatedly and blood trickled down her fingers. Hopefully, she wouldn't hit an artery and do Daniels's dirty work for him by bleeding to death.

"You're willing to kill just to cover up a lie on a financial statement?"

"That lie could keep me from getting reelected."

"And to keep me quiet, you're willing to commit murder?"

"Running this town is a power to which I've become accustomed. Believe me, I never wanted to kill you. But after you found the note in the bottom of Andrew's box, I knew you wouldn't keep quiet," he said with a sly glance in her direction.

"How did you know about the incriminating evidence against you?"

"The man in the van has been following you for some time. After he saw you find those notes, I knew I had to kill you. And I'm going after Wade next."

*Oh, God.* He was insane. He'd actually had someone following her, although no one appeared to be following now. Her heart pounded and her mouth went dry with fear. "You can't keep killing people." She said the words to keep him talking, to keep him distracted from her leaning forward to ease the pressure against her wrists.

"What do you mean by people? You'll only be my second victim. It's a shame really. Who would have thought that I would have to do away with a pretty young thing like you. Politics really does make strange bedfellows."

Daniels's voice was cheery, as if he were discussing his summer vacation plans or his advertising scheme to be Mustang Valley's repeat mayor. His tone increased her determination to free her hands. But when the tie finally snapped free, she was unprepared to make her next move.

The scissors weren't big enough to do much damage but they were the only weapon she had. She gripped them tightly behind her back and worked out the numbness in her wrists. Now what? Reach over and wrestle him for the wheel? Should she force the car off the road? There was no guarantee either of them would survive, but at least she had a chance of taking him with her—if she crashed the car.

Oh, God.

She told herself the only way she could protect Daniels from coming after the ones she loved was to grab the steering wheel and yank hard. But she didn't want to die.

She couldn't imagine the pain she would cause her parents if she died. And Wade. He might not have admitted having feelings for her—but she had them for him. She wanted the time to explore where their relationship could go. She wanted more days, more nights. Right now she desperately wanted just a minute in his arms.

But she had no time.

Daniels was taking her to Wade's ranch. Once he slowed down, the possibility of her crashing the car lessened. She had to make her move now while they sped down the highway. This part of Texas didn't have many trees.

And they'd passed the last overpass and bridge abutment several miles back. The telephone poles flashed by too fast for her to aim at one of them. But a billboard was coming up on the right. A billboard with steel-poled, solid legs.

She wedged the scissors into her left hand, crooked her thumb over the edge. Every muscle in her arms and shoulders tensed as she waited for the perfect moment. She saw no cars up ahead. Just one pair of headlights a long ways back.

*You can do this.*

*On three.*

*One.*

*Two.*

*Three!*

She slid her hand with the scissors out from behind her back. And she stabbed Daniels' thigh.

He shouted in pain.

The car swerved, knocking into a low wooden fence she hadn't noticed. Fence slats flew into the sky.

Kelly released the scissors and yanked on the steering wheel. Daniels cursed. Shoved her away.

Damn it. They were going to miss the steel poles. Then the car hit a ditch and toppled over.

WADE COULDN'T BE CERTAIN Kelly was in the car he was following. When he'd entered Dot's café and Kelly hadn't been out front, he'd assumed she'd gone to the ladies' room. However, when he'd heard insistent honking from the street out back, he'd hurriedly knocked on the ladies' room door, then checked inside.

No one was there.

And his adrenaline kicked into overdrive. He shoved out the back exit just in time to see a vehicle's taillights making a hard right.

Wade had rushed back inside the restaurant. Neither Dot nor the waitress could tell him Kelly's whereabouts. They thought she'd left with Cara and Lindsey but couldn't be sure. He tried to phone Cara but voice mail answered at the *Mustang Gazette.* He hung up and tried Lindsey at the office. But it was almost midnight. No one answered and he didn't have her home phone number.

While he called information, he unlocked the Jag, drove around the block and searched for the taillights he'd seen disappearing at the corner. Fifteen minutes later he still hadn't caught up with the car he was following. Still unsure if Kelly was in that car, he didn't consider turning around. One thing he knew for sure, the car up ahead of him was traveling at a high rate of speed and the driver didn't want to be caught.

Wade tried Cara at home again—no answer. If Kelly was still with her friends and they'd gone off together without Kelly telling him, he was going to be both relieved and angry at her for putting him through this gut-stabbing fear for her safety.

She probably wasn't in the car he was tailing. And yet, suppose she was?

He pressed the pedal down on the Jag and sped along the country highway. At least he knew the road and its curves well, since he used this route on the way to his property. Up ahead the car careened onto the shoulder of the road, then veered back in a zigzag pattern.

Was the driver drunk? Or was a struggle going on inside the car?

Were his instincts on target? The car rolled over and skidded into the billboard's foundation. He swallowed his panic, jammed on his brakes and ran to the smoking car, which had ended in an upright position.

The sight of Kelly on the passenger side made his heart pound and his mouth go dry with fear. She wasn't moving. And he could smell gasoline amid the smoke.

Yanking open the door, he reached inside, turned the key to switch off the engine and pulled Kelly out. Her eyes were closed. Blood trickled down her forehead. He didn't stop to see whether she was still breathing or had a pulse. He had to get her away from the car before the flames reached the gasoline tank and the vehicle exploded.

Sick with worry, Wade carried her about a hundred yards, sank into the grass, ready to go back for the driver. But the car, whose engine he'd turned off, suddenly revved. The driver must be conscious. But what the hell?

The driver should be getting out of the car, racing from the flames. Instead the idiot was driving, turning.

Aiming straight for them.

Wade didn't hesitate. He scooped Kelly back into his arms, searched for cover. There was none. Except maybe he could place the Jag between him and the oncoming car.

He had only seconds and strained to sprint with Kelly in his arms. His lungs burned in the smoky air. His thighs stung with the effort. Clutching her tightly to his chest, he vowed that if they couldn't both get away, at the last moment he'd thrust her to safety or die trying.

Behind him he could hear the vehicle gaining on him. But he didn't spare a second to look back. He dived behind the Jag, twisting in the air to cushion Kelly as the two of them hit the dirt.

The fall seemed to jar her awake. Her eyes opened and stared at him puzzled. ''What—'' Then he could see memories wash over her. ''The mayor—''

The mayor? Wade spied Daniels turning the car around to make another pass at running over them. Smoke belching from the undercarriage didn't seem to slow him down.

''Can you get inside the Jag?'' Wade asked Kelly, unsure of her medical condition. She had an assortment of scrapes and bruises but no obvious broken bones. However, after that crash she could have sustained a multitude of internal ailments.

She scrambled awkwardly, and he could tell she was hurting, but she made it inside. She slammed the door shut, then reached inside the glove compartment and pulled out her gun.

Wade started the powerful engine. Too late.

From his left the other vehicle slammed into them hard enough to shatter the driver's window. Kelly fired two shots.

He had no idea if the window had broken from the collision or her bullets, didn't know if she'd hit anything at all, but the gunfire must have frightened the mayor enough to reconsider trying to crash into them again. Daniels roared back onto the highway and sped away in the opposite direction from Mustang Valley.

"Go after him," Kelly demanded, her tone commanding, urgent.

The moment Wade pressed his foot to the gas pedal, he realized he wasn't attaining full power. "Something's wrong."

"He's getting away." Kelly peered down the road, seemingly unconcerned by the blood trickling down her forehead and cheek. "We have to go—"

The Jag's engine died.

Wade shoved open his door, exited the vehicle and hurried toward the engine, but he couldn't open the hood due to the damage from the collision. Without tools he probably couldn't have done much, anyway.

"We aren't going anywhere. But we can call for

reinforcements.'' Wade flipped open his new car phone and dialed Deputy Mitch Warwick.

"Do you know what time it is?" answered a cranky Mitch.

"Mayor Daniels just kidnapped Kelly McGovern, then tried to run us both over."

"What!"

"Wake up. Even as we speak the mayor is heading due south. My guess it that he doesn't plan to stop until after he crosses the Mexican border."

"Is this a joke?"

"Mayor Daniels admitted to me that he killed Andrew," Kelly pitched in.

"What was his motive?" Mitch asked, the sleepiness now gone from his voice.

While Kelly explained that the nondisclosure of his ownership in some land deal coming to light could have prevented the mayor from winning his reelection campaign, Wade looked her over. He'd been so afraid when he couldn't find her at Dot's. Then he'd watched the car roll over, and when he'd run from the smoking car and danger, he'd been ready to plant himself between her and Daniels's car to protect her.

No woman had ever meant so much to him.

And now as she stood in the smoky field after having almost died twice in the last few minutes, all he could do was marvel at her inner strength. She'd fired two shots at the mayor, then, after almost being run over, she'd urged him to chase Daniels down.

Another woman would have been clinging to him, crying, hiding. But she'd been determined to fight for the justice she wanted for her brother, and he suspected her determination might have even been responsible for the initial crash into that billboard foundation. All in all, Kelly McGovern was quite a woman.

Mitch promised to send an ambulance and backup. He said Sheriff Wilson and his deputies would find Mayor Daniels and bring him back to Mustang Valley for justice. Wade figured with the smoke coming out of that car, finding the mayor wouldn't be too difficult.

Kelly hung up the phone and swore. "Damn. Damn. Damn."

Wade hurried to her side, ready to grab her if she toppled over. "What's wrong? Are you hurt?"

"I'm bleeding." She touched the blood on her chin as if she hadn't realized she'd been hurt until just that moment.

"You're going to be fine," he tried to reassure her. "It's just a small cut."

"I'm bleeding on my silk *blouse*. The stain is never going to come out."

He stared at her, his lower jaw dropping in astonishment. "You're worried about your blouse?"

"It's a Donna Karan."

"How terrible." Wade smacked his forehead in mock horror.

"The stain won't come out."

She glared at him, the gun by her side, pointed at the dirt. "Are you making fun of me?"

He held up his hands in surrender and teased. "Not while you have the gun."

Her eyebrows narrowed. "What—"

The sound of a loud boom cut off her words.

## Chapter Fourteen

Ambulances, sirens blaring, a fire truck and several deputies in their cars rushed down the road. One black-and-white pulled beside them and stopped. Deputy Warwick exited his vehicle. "Are you two all right?"

"Yeah, but after the explosion we just heard, I'm not so sure about Mayor Daniels." Wade's tone was thoughtful, and all his earlier teasing had disappeared from his demeanor. He stood straight, his face smudged from the smoke, his shirt spattered with her blood, and to Kelly he'd never looked more beautiful. Men weren't supposed to be beautiful but Wade Lansing was beautiful to her. She didn't think she'd ever tire of looking at him.

He'd saved her life, risked his own to rescue her. Without his strength, quick thinking and courage, she might not be standing there right now. Odd how he could commit himself to her with actions but couldn't follow through with words. While she had difficulty understanding where he was coming from, she knew he hadn't had a loving childhood. He might not even recognize how he felt about her, and it could be a long time, if ever, before he could give her what she wanted from him.

And as much as she loved him, she couldn't spend her life waiting for him to make the first move. She wasn't ready to give up on him, either, not after what they'd shared. So, just as she'd seduced him, she would have to lead him to the idea that they could be a permanent couple. Only, she didn't know how to get there from here.

She must have missed some of the conversation between Wade and Deputy Warwick because suddenly his radio blared with information.

"The mayor's vehicle exploded," a deputy reported. "Mayor Daniels is dead. No one else is injured here, but we could use the ambulance to take the body back to town."

"So it's over." Wade took her hand, and then she flew into his arms. His powerful chest supported her, his strong arms closed around her. She'd wanted justice for Andrew and she'd gotten that. But along the way she'd found something else. She'd found the love of her life. The other details could wait. Right now she just wanted Wade to take her home.

Apparently that wasn't going to happen: Her parents drove up and came rushing over.

She hugged both her mother and father to assure them that she was safe. At the same time she wanted to bring Wade into their circle of love. But when she tugged his hand, he resisted.

Standing tall and alone, he spoke with the deputy about towing the Jag back to town. He told her he would hitch a ride with Mitch to give them a run-down of what had happened and suggested she go home with her folks.

If he thought he could get rid of her that easily, he was so wrong. However, now was not the time to have a personal discussion, with all the medical people, Mitch and her folks around.

Tomorrow morning she would give a detailed report to Sheriff Wilson and then she intended to meet with the girls for a plan-of-action session. By the time she was done with Wade Lansing, he wouldn't know what had hit him.

WADE WATCHED KELLY get into the car with her parents. He made himself keep watching as she drove away and wondered at the sense of loss that gripped him. He would see her tomorrow when she came to his house to pick up her things, but he was accustomed to her living at his house, sharing their evenings together.

Hell. He had a business to run. With the investigation over and Daniels dead, she no longer needed his protection. She would be safe with her folks. So why did her leaving him feel so wrong? Why did he have this hollow ache in his chest as if he was making the biggest mistake of his life?

After hitching a ride with Mitch to his ranch, Wade cleaned up in his shower and headed to the Hit 'Em Again, where not even the business details of ordering supplies, hiring a new bartender and paying bills could totally distract him from missing Kelly and worrying about her. By closing time, he'd worked himself up and used his excess energy on a three-mile run back home.

Tomorrow, he'd take care of purchasing another truck, now that the insurance company had come through. He kept checking his cell phone for messages, but there were none. Which meant that Kelly was fine. In her own home, her own bed—back where she belonged.

Wade settled into his hot tub on his back deck, hoping the heat would soothe his thoughts. But he could have sworn he smelled Kelly's unique scent, recalled how she'd soaked in this exact spot, teasing him with her sensuality, taunting him to take one forbidden taste. One taste had led to another and their lovemaking had been so powerful that he would remember her for the rest of his days—and some very long nights.

It was his own fault, of course. He should have resisted her sweet seduction. He should never have even kissed her.

Damn it. He should be satisfied that Kelly was safe and back in her protected world. Andrew would be pleased with their resourcefulness and that they'd both survived. And especially that his killer had been revealed and had paid for the crime with his own life.

Wade should be exhausted after the trying day they'd spent, but he was wide awake. And as he watched the sun rise up over the horizon, the angry streaks of purple and slashes of pink reminded him today would be harder than yesterday.

When his cell phone shrilled, it startled him so much that he almost knocked it onto the ground. The voice on the line was female—but not Kelly's, not the woman whose voice he'd been hoping to hear.

"Sorry to call so early."

"Who is this?"

"Debbie West."

Why was she calling *him* when Kelly had given Debbie *her* number. "What's wrong?"

"The McGoverns aren't answering their phone."

He quickly filled Debbie in about Mayor Daniels and their stressful evening. "They might have just turned off their phone to get a good night's sleep, or maybe it doesn't ring in the bedrooms."

"You're probably right."

"But?" he prodded, not yet too concerned.

"Niles tracked me down to the women's shelter where I've been staying."

"Women's shelter? With all the money Kelly gave you why aren't you at a hotel?"

"Niles has a violent temper. I felt safer here after he tracked me to my new apartment I'd rented in the middle of the night. He was ranting about Mayor Daniels's death and how he could lose everything."

All along Wade and Kelly had suspected that Niles might have been backing the mayor's election, that Niles might have been helping Daniels with some of his dirty work—but suppose it was the other way around? Suppose the mayor had been taking orders from the powerful oil man? That would mean Kelly still might not be safe.

"What do you mean, he could lose everything?"

"I don't know the details, but he borrowed a lot of money and he was counting on a big payoff with a deal he had with the mayor. With his empire about to crash, if this all ends up in the newspaper, I'm worried about him trying to silence Kelly so it can never go to trial.''

Looked like he'd have to fire up the old Caddy after all. ''I'll try Kelly on the cell phone on my way over to the McGoverns' house.''

But the moment Wade opened his front door to leave, Niles was standing there pointing a gun at him and sneering. ''We're most definitely going to call your girlfriend.''

And Wade no longer needed a lab report to verify that the paint from Niles's car would prove he'd killed Johnny Dixon.

EXHAUSTED, KELLY SLEPT soundly and still only half-awake, she reached groggily for the ringing cell phone. ''Hello?''

''Kelly, it's Wade. Don't—''

At the sound of a loud thunk, Kelly jerked wide awake, fear and confusion washing away her sleepiness. ''Wade? Wade! Answer me.''

She heard several grunts and flicked on her light. It was 7:00 a.m. and her heart pounded with terror as her phone transmitted the clear and sickening smacks of a fist striking flesh. Grunts. Curses.

*Oh, God.*

She raised her fist to her mouth and bit down on a knuckle. Wade was in trouble. He'd tried to call her, and someone must have jumped him. From the sound of the fight, he was taking a terrible beating and from that she could conclude only one thing: Someone had taken him by surprise and he was no longer in a position to fight back.

She had to do something.

Kelly was reaching for the house phone to dial 911 when a man spoke to her over the phone in a familiar voice she almost recognized. "I have your boyfriend tied to a chair. He doesn't look so pretty anymore." She'd thought she'd been hearing a fight, but in reality what she'd heard was Wade being hit as he sat helpless, and her stomach roiled. "If you ever want to see Wade Lansing alive again, you must do exactly as I say."

"How do I know he's still alive?" she asked, making her tone careless and hard, hoping to counter her trembling from scalp to toes. Despite her fear, she had to stay calm. Stalling for time, she wondered what she should do and how she could best help Wade.

"You just heard Wade talking to you, didn't you?" the man growled with a biting sarcasm that told her to be very careful what she said and how she said it. As much as she wanted to sob, she suspected this man would only respect strength.

"I also heard you hitting him," she countered as she slipped on a shirt and a pair of jeans.

"Well, Wade wanted to play hero. He didn't want to sweet-talk you into coming to rescue him. And I don't have time to change his mind."

She suddenly recognized the voice. Niles! She was almost positive. And her recognition triggered other thoughts. What was Niles doing with Wade and why was he beating him?

Desperately trying not to think of Wade lying somewhere unconscious and injured and vulnerable, her thoughts raced to the conclusion that Niles must have been not just backing the mayor's reelection campaign but working with Daniels. Niles wouldn't want public scrutiny of his business dealings with the mayor, and with his empire on the verge of collapse, he, too, might be willing to commit murder to protect his secrets. The paint on that dented car probably matched Johnny Dixon's. And if Niles would attempt to kill Dixon, there was no reason he would spare Wade.

In the background Wade yelled, "Don't listen to him."

She heard another nauseating smack, then gagging, and Niles returned to the phone, breathing heavily. "We haven't the time for ridiculous heroics. You get your pretty little ass over to your boyfriend's house, right now."

So he could kill both of them? As much as she feared for Wade's safety she had to make the right decision. Getting herself killed by foolishly running to his side wouldn't help either of them.

She should wake her folks. Call the sheriff. She made her voice sound much younger and girlish. "I'm scared, and besides I don't have a car. Mine was wrecked."

"Don't play games with me, woman. Look out your window."

"What?"

"Just do it."

She peeked through the miniblinds and spied a man smoking a cigarette in the front seat of a dark van parked across the neighborhood street. In the first light of dawn she could see him stare directly at her as he tipped his cap.

Niles, not the mayor, was having her watched, and

a shiver crawled down her spine. Clearly the two of them had been working together, since both of them had used the man in the van to spy on her. And since she could tie the mayor to attempted murder, even if Niles had been innocent, just his business dealing with a killer could put the nail in the coffin of his crumbling empire. He couldn't afford to let her live.

"My boy will report back to me if you don't follow my instructions exactly."

"What do you want?"

"Take your daddy's car and meet us at Wade's house. If you try to call anyone or make an extra stop along the way, I'll know, and your boyfriend will be history. You've got ten minutes."

"Make it twenty. I'm not dressed," she lied, but a plan was beginning to form in her mind, a plan that would take a few precious minutes to implement.

Niles chuckled. "Fifteen and not a minute more, or I shoot your friend. Got it?"

"I'm scared." Kelly unzipped her jeans and slipped them off. She went to her closet and thumbed through her choices, looking for one particular denim jumper with huge wide-angled pockets. "Can't we work this out like adults? My daddy's a wealthy man, he'd be willing to pay—"

Niles hung up the phone. Apparently, he wasn't interested in a deal—which could only mean one thing. He intended to kill both Wade and her, no matter what.

Kelly didn't dare use her phone, and tossed it on the bed to free her hand up to dress quickly. Niles might have planted some kind of listening device in her room, or on her clothing, or in her purse. She couldn't risk his man overhearing her—but that didn't prevent her from scribbling a fast and furious note to her folks. She slipped the jumper that she normally wore belted at the waist over her head and glanced at herself in the mirror. Not the effect she needed.

Perhaps a blouse under the jumper would portray the helpless little-girl effect she was going for. Much better. At least she needn't bother with makeup to pull off her deception. Then she parted her hair down the middle, braided each side and tied the braids off with pink ribbons. She slipped white socks on her feet, folded them down to the ankles and tied on an old pair of sneakers. On the way out the door she grabbed her gun and made sure it was loaded.

Not the place to hurry.

She made herself turn back and check her image again in the mirror. Without the belt, the jumper hung loosely and eclipsed her curves. The huge pocket, which now held her loaded gun that she'd grabbed from the floor of the Jag before the tow truck had hauled it off didn't give her much security.

Last but not least, she slipped a note under her parents' door on her way down the hall and banged on their door. She checked her watch, her heart beating so fast that she felt as if she'd just run a mile.

Breathe.

She needed to remain sharp, not tire herself out by tensing every muscle. In retrospect she should have told Niles that she wouldn't come into the house until he proved to her that Wade was still alive. And that mistake might cost her.

She had no time to second-guess herself. No time for regrets. But her biggest fear was that Niles might not keep Wade alive until she got there.

When she pulled her dad's Mercedes out of the driveway and headed out of the subdivision, the van followed her all the way out of town. She did nothing to attract attention to herself, driving the speed limit on the mostly deserted streets. She didn't want to risk doing anything that would cause the van's driver to report to Niles that she wasn't exactly following his instructions.

She parked the car in the driveway. Now what?

Slowly she exited the car, unobtrusively checking the pocket, then deciding to put her hand into the pocket so she could clutch the gun's handle.

"Come right in through the front door." The door opened, but she couldn't see Niles, just his arm.

She hesitated. "I'm not coming inside until I hear Wade's voice."

"Get out of here," Wade shouted, clearly furious that she hadn't listened to him earlier and that she had no intention of listening to him now.

"Satisfied?" Niles asked through the propped-open door.

She wished she could see past the front door so she had some idea of Wade's condition and what kind of situation she was about to walk into. She recalled a Shotgun Sally pillow that her mother had embroidered that said, "Sometimes one must trust oneself."

This was one of those times. She took a deep breath, hoping the added oxygen would not just give her courage but make her wise. Slowly, her heart tip-toeing up her throat, she walked into a certain trap.

WADE CURSED THE BONDS that tied him to the chair, cursed at fate that had let Niles surprise him, cursed at Kelly for stubbornly putting herself in danger. Though his right eye was swollen shut, he could still see out of the left, and Kelly walking through that door almost gave him a heart attack.

How could she be stupid enough to put herself in danger? Was she so naive that she believed Niles wouldn't kill them both? Was she so trusting that she thought she could talk Niles out of his plan?

The bonds that kept his hands firmly tied behind his back and to a chair only served to increase the rage and fear for Kelly that swept through him. She didn't belong in his house, putting herself in danger. And she most certainly didn't belong...in those clothes.

And what the hell had she done to her hair? He tried to blink the blood from his good eye. She'd braided her hair and had dressed herself like a little girl.

Damn. Damn. Damn.

She had dressed herself to pander to Niles's twisted tastes of young flesh, and at the moment of realization, the hot rage inside him froze icy cold. He licked at the cut of his swollen lip, trying to put moisture back into his mouth.

Kelly walked into his living room with the mincing steps of a child, yet just for a moment he caught her vivid blue eyes that glinted with the ferocity of a tigress protecting her mate. Obviously, she had a plan. And no way was Wade going to talk her out of it now, especially after she'd seen the gun Niles had pointed at his head.

The fact that the gun was pointed at Wade and not her didn't make him feel one whit better. Niles would kill him, then Kelly, and the only good thing was that Wade wouldn't have to watch her die. He would never see the life flow out of her or see her drop lifeless to the floor.

What was her plan? Even if she had somehow managed to bring help, she shouldn't have placed herself in danger.

But she was here, and he'd do his best to help, although what that would be, with his hands and feet tied, he had no idea. All of these thoughts had raced with warp speed, and Kelly had yet to come fully inside the living area.

"Shut the door behind you," Niles ordered.

"Okay." She did as he asked, and then Niles flipped on the light.

When Kelly turned back and saw Wade's battered face, she gasped. Her face whitened, and a muscle ticked at her throat. "I thought we could come to some kind of agreement."

"Don't do this," Wade pleaded, earning himself a slap across the face that opened the cut above his good eye.

"What kind of agreement do you plan to make after taking paint samples of my car?" Niles asked her, the gun still pointed at Wade's head.

"Whatever kind you'd like," Kelly responded in a frightened-little-girl voice that should have made Niles suspicious.

What was she doing? Surely she didn't think that Niles would accept her instead of Debbie?

Niles chuckled. "I can get what you're offering anywhere."

"Maybe. Maybe not. I thought what you wanted was to shut me up. Forever. Well, even if you kill both of us, that's not possible. However, if you let us live, perhaps we could make a deal."

Wade shook his head, as much out of frustration as to clear the blood from his eye. "You can't bargain with a man who won't keep his word."

Niles kicked his leg.

"Stop that." Kelly walked toward Niles, but she'd changed her angle slightly, making it impossible for the oil man to keep the gun directly on Wade and watch her at the same time.

Wade fought to keep the blood from blocking his vision, and his gaze dropped to Kelly's hand, which had slipped inside the roomy denim pocket of her dress. Did that pocket bulge more than it should have from just her hand?

Wade didn't know. Fear for her made him lunge against the chair, tipping it over, slamming him onto the floor. He almost blacked out, fought against the stars exploding in his head.

A shot ricocheted nearby, landed on the floor, shooting splinters into his neck. That shot was followed by two more.

Wade tensed, expecting pain, but none came.

He heard a body thud to the floor.

"Kelly?"

"I'm right here." Her hands tugged on the ropes

to untie his hands, and she was sobbing. "I shot the son of a bitch right between the eyes."

Suddenly he was free and gathering her into his arms. "Are you all right?"

"I had to come." Her chest heaved and tears rained down her cheeks. He cuddled her against his chest, turning her away from Niles' very dead body. "I had no choice. I couldn't let him kill you."

He rocked her as she cried. "You almost scared me to death coming here when I told you not to."

"I'm not very good at...taking orders. You'll have to let me make it up to you."

She wanted to make it up to him? She'd risked her life to save him and she wanted his forgiveness? He would never understand her. Never.

But so what? He didn't have to understand her. He only had to love her.

He loved her.

Of course he loved her. How could he not have the courage to admit that to himself after the bravery she'd exhibited today.

He loved her.

But the way he saw it, that meant it was going to be harder to let her go. Kelly McGovern had big things to do with her life and important places to go. He would not be the one responsible for holding her back, for saddling her with a brood of kids that would prevent her from attaining her goals.

He loved her.

And that meant that no matter how much pain it caused him, he had to set her free.

## Chapter Fifteen

"Wade hasn't even called me in a week," Kelly complained to Cara and Lindsey over lunch at Dot's sandwich shop.

Cara held up a sour dill pickle and pointed it at Kelly. "Phones work both ways, you know."

Kelly sighed. "I always get his machine."

"Why don't you go over to the Hit 'Em Again Saloon?" Lindsey suggested. "The bar might be his turf, but he won't want to run out the door to avoid you in front of his employees."

"I've considered that plan." Kelly bit into her BLT on toasted rye, chewed and swallowed. "The Hit 'Em Again is not the place to have a private conversation."

"You know what your problem is?" Cara said.

Kelly dabbed a smudge of mayonnaise from her lip. "That I've fallen in love with a man so stubborn he won't admit that he's wrong?"

Cara shook her head.

Kelly tried again. "That I'm not willing to let go of the best thing that's ever happened to me?"

Cara rolled her eyes at the ceiling, and Lindsey

laughed, then tried to smother her reaction with a cough. She ended up almost choking, and Kelly had to pound her on the back. "You okay?"

"I'm fine."

Cara stole the pickle off of Kelly's plate. "Your problem is that you are just as stubborn as he is."

Kelly frowned at the pickle. "Hey, I was going to eat that."

Cara grinned and crunched happily. "Too late."

"And I'm not stubborn."

Lindsey chuckled again. "Yes, you are. You won't give up and he won't give in. You're a perfect match."

"Wade doesn't see it that way." Kelly shoved the second half of her sandwich at Cara. "Here, you might as well have this, too. I've lost my appetite."

"Thanks." Cara tugged Kelly's plate closer. "Your problem is that you want Wade to talk to you."

"Well, duh."

"You're thinking like a woman," Cara added between bites of the BLT.

"I *am* a woman."

"What's your point?" Lindsey asked with a frown.

"Tell us, what's your ultimate goal?" Cara prodded.

Kelly had had more than enough time to think about her answer in the past few days. "A life with Wade. Marriage."

"Now you're talking," Cara said.

"Excuse me? Have you forgotten the man won't even speak to me?"

"Talk isn't what's important here."

"It's not?" Bewildered, Kelly looked at her friend, wondering if she'd put in too many hours of overtime lately, because Cara certainly wasn't making sense. Cara had interviewed Johnny Dixon in his hospital bed and written a page-two story in the *Mustang Gazette* about how Niles Deagen had run him off the road because he'd overheard an incriminating conversation between Niles and the former mayor. Page one had been about the mayor's and Niles's deaths.

"You need to take action," Cara insisted.

"And what, pray tell, would you have me do?"

"I don't know." Cara polished off the last of Kelly's sandwich and washed it down with a glass of sweet tea. "Trying to talk to the man isn't getting you anywhere, so you need to change tactics. Act. Do something."

"Sneak into his bed and seduce him?" Lindsey suggested.

"She already did that. She needs to do something more drastic," Cara prodded.

Kelly had the feeling that Cara was leading her down a twisting, narrow road with a steep cliff that she could easily fall off. Cara had a plan. She clearly just wanted Kelly to think that it was her own idea.

"Think of a Shotgun Sally legend," Cara hinted.

"Which one? There are so many of them, we have no idea which ones are fiction."

"Who cares about the truth? Pick one that will work for you."

"Well, you know that I'm partial to one particular legend about my illustrious ancestor, but do you want me to point a rifle at Wade and force him to say his wedding vows?''

Cara signaled her with a thumbs-up. "Now, there's a bold idea worthy of page one."

Cara was still smarting that she hadn't been assigned to write about the mayor's death. But that didn't mean she had to help create the news before she reported it. And urging Kelly to kidnap Wade at gunpoint and force him in front of a justice of the peace might have worked two centuries ago, but not in this day and age.

"Uh-hem." Lindsey went into attorney mode. "May I remind you ladies that holding a gun on a man except in self-defense is not legal?"

"At least I have one sane friend," Kelly muttered, because Cara's suggestion had kicked her pulse up a notch. Her thoughts raced at the appealing and oh-so-outrageous idea. "Suppose I don't point the gun at him? Just carry it."

"That would be an implied threat," Lindsey stated, "and the law starts getting sticky there."

"The gun needn't be loaded, either," Cara pointed out with a twinkle in her eyes.

Kelly glanced from Cara to Lindsey and shook her head. "I don't know. This is insane."

"Do you think Wade is going to let you threaten him into marriage if it's really against his will?" Lindsey asked pointedly.

No, he would not.

And that's when Kelly had her answer. No more mooning around and waiting for Wade to call. No more sleepless nights wishing she was back in his bed. She was going to act and act boldly. After all, it was in her genes.

She kissed each of her friends on the cheek. "Thanks. You are the best. Wish me luck." She stood from the table, suddenly sure of herself.

"Where are you going?" Cara grumbled. "You didn't even taste your dessert."

"You go ahead." Kelly hurried out the door. "I'm going shopping."

"Of course she is." Cara placed a forkful of cheesecake into her mouth and grinned at Lindsey. "Have you ever noticed that after Kelly goes shopping, there's always fireworks afterward in Mustang Valley?"

"WADE LANSING, you open this door right now," Kelly demanded in a voice that he couldn't fail to recognize.

"Okay. Okay. Don't break down the damn door." Grumpy after a late night at the Hit 'Em Again, grumpier still from missing Kelly and several sleepless nights, Wade padded to his front door barefoot, knowing that another encounter with her would set back his recovery for days.

What was she doing here? He didn't want a reminder of how good she looked first thing in the morning. Or how sweet she smelled after her shower. Or what that smile of hers did to heat him to a fever pitch.

What was she doing here so early in the morning? It figured that she'd wake him up ten minutes after he'd finally fallen asleep. But then nothing about Kelly was convenient. Not the fact that she was Andrew's sister. Most definitely not the fact that even when he closed his eyes he saw her in his dreams. Certainly not the fact that she probably wanted to be around him because it made her feel closer to the brother she had lost. And absolutely not the fact that he wanted her more than he'd ever wanted any woman in his life.

For the first time he admitted to himself the real reason for pushing her away. He was scared. Scared that she would abandon him or die on him, just like every other person who he'd ever counted on. That might not be fair or rational but it was the way he felt.

However, just because he loved her didn't necessarily mean he wanted the torture of seeing her in the flesh. His dreams and memories were vivid enough, thank you very much. Nevertheless, he unlocked his door and kicked it open.

And got the shock of his life.

Kelly stood there in a creamy white lace wedding dress. Her lush breasts filled the bodice, and the early-morning sunlight accentuated a glistening blush on her cheeks and a tantalizing blush in the hollows. Not even the shotgun cocked at her side could dispel the image of her loveliness that made his mouth go dry.

"You...are wearing...a wedding gown."

"How observant of you." Kelly's rich laughter woke him right up and convinced him that he wasn't dreaming. Not even his dreams were this imaginative. Or vivid.

She brushed by him, close enough for him to take in the fascinating scent of spiced lemons with a hint of strawberry. The view from the back was as enticing as her front. The dress swooped low in back, emphasizing her smooth skin, and his breath hitched in his chest.

He didn't want to react to her, but who was he kidding? He had no choice, and his tone came out much huskier than he would have liked. "What do you want?"

"You." She planted the gun handle on the floor and steadied herself with the barrel, cocking one hip at a sexy angle that reminded him of Charlie's Angels. "So we can do this the easy way or the hard way."

"You can't just barge into my house—"

"You let me in," she said so reasonably that he just knew she was up to one of her tricks.

"—and brandish a weapon."

"I'm not brandishing, I'm leaning."

"And the difference is…?"

"Doesn't matter—except in a court of law."

He raised a skeptical eyebrow. "Isn't it a little late to be worried about the law?"

"Huh?" For the first time she seemed confused.

And he had to admit just to himself that sparring with her was much more fun than sleeping and dreaming about her. He allowed a glimmer of appreciation to show on his face. "The way you're dressed you could be arrested for all kinds of things."

"Oh, really?"

"Like getting married without a license."

"I'd like to see you tell that to a judge."

"Okay."

He frowned at her. She'd just given in way too easily. "What do you mean, okay?"

"Okay, as in *yes.* Let's go talk to the judge."

"What are you talking about?"

"You're impossible. I want to get married."

Uh-oh. He'd walked right into that one. He could tell she'd set him up by the pleased gleam of satisfaction in her eyes.

"Where's the groom?" he teased, his pulse racing, because he suddenly knew that he could do this. When Kelly set her mind to something, she didn't change it. When she said forever, she meant it. She wouldn't change her mind or leave him and his mind suddenly cleared like a defroster evaporating fog from a window. He could have her. All he had to do was take the biggest leap of faith in his life.

"I'm looking at the groom."

She wanted to marry him—not have a summer fling. She couldn't have shocked him more if she'd claimed she wanted to enter a convent.

She wanted to marry him. That meant he could have her for a lifetime, not just a few lousy weeks of the summer. That meant she never planned to leave him. Marriage was permanent.

She wanted to marry him, and his heart hummed with joy.

He folded his arms across his chest, thinking hard. "Well, it takes the consent of both parties to get married."

"That's why I brought the gun."

He didn't want to ask if it was loaded. He didn't want to know.

His legs seemed to have gone to jelly and he slid onto the sofa. "We can't get married."

"Sure we can. I got the license yesterday." She sauntered over to him, her hips swaying due to those too-sexy heels. She reached into her bra, removed a piece of folded paper and offered it to him. "After patching you up, Doc already had a sample of your blood."

He marveled at her ingenuity, stunned, shocked and almost stupefied. "And?"

"And nothing." She nudged him with the rifle. "Let's go elope."

Damn, he loved her. When she got all sexy and vulnerable and mad at the same time, she was the most adorable woman. Of course, he had no intention of telling her that—not with her caressing that gun barrel as if it were her best friend. He could think of much better things to do than die of a gunshot wound.

"I can't elope right now," he teased her, but pretended to be deadly serious.

"Why not?"

"My slacks are too tight."

She glanced down at him and chuckled. "I suppose we could take care of that big problem first."

He grabbed her hand and yanked her down beside him. "Good. But we have a few other things to work out." He planted a kiss by her ear. "If we get married, you aren't giving up law school for me."

"If I give up law school, it won't be for you. But I've been considering a career in real estate. I just haven't decided yet."

"And no babies until you finish school."

"You want kids?" she smoothed her hands over his chest and let them dip below his waist.

"Yeah, but not yet." He wrapped an arm around her shoulder, tugged her close and then tipped up her chin to claim her lips. "First, I'm going to let you spoil me in the manner to which I've become accustomed."

"Yes, sir," she teased. "I can tell exactly who is going to be in charge of this marriage."

"You?"

She kissed him and then pulled back. "Oh, did I happen to mention that my wedding veil and your suit are in the car and that the judge is expecting us at noon. The plane leaves for our honeymoon in Hawaii at three. So quit wasting time. Unless you have a better idea?"

He kissed her lips. "Well, there seems to be one important thing you forgot."

"Hmm?"

"You didn't give me time to say I love you."

"That's perfectly okay." She grinned at him. "I already knew that."

\*   \*   \*   \*   \*

*Turn the page for a sneak preview
of the next gripping*
SHOTGUN SALLYS *title,*
Legally Binding
*by rising star Ann Voss Peterson,
on sale in August 2006 in Silhouette Intrigue…*

# Legally Binding

### by

### Ann Voss Peterson

Bart Rawlins forced one eye open. Late-morning sun slanted through his bedroom window, blinding him. Pain, sharper than his old Buck knife, drilled into his skull. He gripped the edge of the mattress and willed the room to stop spinning.

He hadn't had that much to drink at Wade Lansing's Hit 'Em Again Saloon last night, had he? Not enough to warrant a hangover like this.

He remembered hitching a ride to the bar with Gary Tuttle, his foreman at the Four Aces Ranch. Remembered wolfing down some of Wade's famous chili and throwing back a few beers. Not enough to make his head feel like it was about to explode. Not enough to make his mouth taste like an animal had crawled in and died.

Damn but he was too old for this. At thirty-five he always thought he would be settled down with a woman he loved, raising sons and daughters to take over the Four Aces Ranch. Instead he was lying in bed with his boots on and a hangover powerful enough to split his skull.

He raised a hand to his forehead. His fingers felt

sticky on his skin. Sticky and moist and smelled like—

His eyes flew open and he jerked up off the mattress. Head throbbing, he stared at his splayed fingers. Something brown coated his hands and settled into the creases of work-worn skin. The same rusty brown flecked his Wranglers.

*Blood.*

What the hell? Had he gotten drunk and picked a fight? Was a well-aimed punch responsible for his throbbing head?

He pushed himself off the bed and stumbled to the bathroom. Peering into the mirror, he checked his face. Although his nose was slightly crooked from a fall off a horse when he was ten, it looked fine. So did the rest of his face. And a quick check of other body parts turned up nothing, either. The blood must have come from the other guy.

The doorbell's chime echoed through the house.

Who the hell could that be? He tried to scan his memory for an appointment this morning, but his sluggish mind balked.

The doorbell rang again. Whoever it was, he wasn't going away.

Bart turned on the water and plunged his hands into the warm stream. He splashed his face, grabbed a towel and headed down the stairs. He'd get rid of whoever it was so he could nurse his hangover in peace. And try to remember what in the hell had happened last night.

He reached the door and yanked it open.

As wide as he was tall, Deputy Hurley Zeller looked up at Bart through narrowed little eyes. The sheriff's right-hand man had a way of staring that made a man feel he'd done something illegal even if he hadn't. And ever since Bart beat him out for quarterback in high school, he'd always saved his best accusing stare for Bart.

Bart shifted his boots on the wood floor. "What's up, Hurley?"

"I had bad news."

Bart rooted his boots to the spot. If he'd learned one thing about bad news in his thirty-five years, it was that it was best to take it like a shot of rot-gut whiskey. Straight up and all at once. "What is it?"

"Your uncle Jebediah. He's dead."

Bart blew a stream of air through tight lips. Uncle Jeb's death meant there would be no reconciliation. No forgiveness to mend the feud in the Rawlins clan that had started the day Bart's granddad died and left Hiriam a larger chunk of the seventy-thousand-acre ranch. Now it was too late for a happy ending to that story. "Well, that is bad news, Hurley. Real bad. How did he die?"

Hurley focused on the leather pouch on Bart's belt, the pouch where he kept his Buck knife. "Maybe I should ask you that question."

Bart draped the towel over one shoulder and moved his hand to the pouch. It was empty. The folding hunting knife he'd hung on his belt since his father gave it to him for his fourteenth birthday was gone. Shock jolted Bart to the soles of his Tony Lamas. "You don't think I killed—" The question lodged in his throat. He followed Hurley's pointed stare to the towel on his shoulder.

The white terrycloth was pink with blood.

A smile spread over Hurley's thin lips. ''I think you're coming with me, Bart. And you've got the right to remain silent.''

LINDSEY WELLINGTON adjusted her navy-blue suit, tucked her Italian leather briefcase under one arm and marched toward the Mustang County Jail and her first solo case. She hadn't been this nervous since she'd taken the Texas bar exam. At least her years at Harvard Law School had given her plenty of experience taking tests, but this was a different story. This was real life.

*This was murder.*

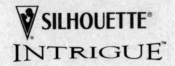

# SILHOUETTE®
# INTRIGUE™

## ROCKY MOUNTAIN MANOEUVRES
### by Cassie Miles
#### Colorado Crime Consultants

PI Adam Briggs wasn't happy that his secretary, Molly Griffith, wanted to pose as an undercover bride to investigate a string of petty thefts. But when the case turned dark and a killer targeted Molly, Adam knew he had to protect the woman he couldn't resist.

## THE STOLEN BRIDE by Jacqueline Diamond

Officer Joseph Lowery had stopped his childhood sweetheart, Erin Marshall, marrying a man she couldn't even remember saying yes to. But now they were dodging bullets together and risking everything—and their only hope is for Erin to unlock her lost memories...

## LEGALLY BINDING by Ann Voss Peterson
#### Shotgun Sallys

Reformed bad boy rancher Bart Rawlins has been accused of a murder he didn't commit and only Texas lawyer Lindsey Wellington could prove it. But trying not to fall for her sexy client was going to be more of a battle than proving Bart was innocent...

## GHOST HORSE by Patricia Rosemoor
#### Eclipse

When her best friend disappeared, Chloe Morgan went undercover to investigate what had really happened. Handsome and mysterious horse breeder Damien Graylord was her first suspect. But then Chloe found herself falling for him, and revealing the truth became a risk she might just need to take.

**On sale from 21st July 2006**

*www.silhouette.co.uk*

0706/18a

# SILHOUETTE
# *Sensation*™

## THE CAPTIVE'S RETURN
### by Catherine Mann

*Wingmen Warriors*

During a hazardous mission, Lieutenant Colonel Lucas
Quade discovered not only that his long-lost wife, Sara, was
alive but that they had a daughter. As they struggled against
the danger all around them, could they reclaim their passion
for each other?

## THE SHEIKH WHO LOVED ME
### by Loreth Anne White

When Sheikh David Rashid found a beautiful amnesiac
washed ashore after a storm, it seemed she held the key to
unlocking his silent daughter. But the secrets buried in
the mysterious woman's memory threatened to destroy
them all…

## MELTING POINT by Debra Cowan

*The Hot Zone*

When Collier McClain and Kiley Russell were teamed up
to uncover a multiple murderer, their initial attraction only
grew deeper. But both were determined to avoid trouble,
so no matter how hot their desire, their vows to keep things
professional had no melting point – or did they?

**On sale from 21st July 2006**

*Available at WHSmith, Tesco, ASDA, Borders, Eason,
Sainsbury's and most bookshops*

*www.silhouette.co.uk*

# HER KIND OF TROUBLE by Evelyn Vaughn

### *Bombshell: The Grail Keepers*

Modern-day grail keeper Maggi Sanger jumped at the chance to go to Egypt in search of another legendary grail. But trouble soon found her. Crime lords, sabotage and old enemies dogged her and, at every turn, the investigation led her back to a very familiar man…

# SECRETS OF THE WOLF by Karen Whiddon

### *The Pack*

Brie Beswich went to Leaning Tree for answers about her mother's death. But all she found was more questions and hints of an ancient secret. The town's handsome sheriff seemed to know more than he was saying. Could Brie trust this mysterious man and the passion that threatened to consume them both?

# THE GOLDEN GIRL by Erica Orloff

### *Bombshell: The IT Girls*

Heiress Madison Taylor-Pruitt had it all—money, looks and her choice of men. But when her own father was named prime suspect in a murder, Madison's future seemed bleak —until the elite Gotham Rose spy ring asked her to find the real killer. Could the savvy socialite stay on the A-list *and* keep her father off the Most-Wanted list?

## On sale from 21st July 2006

*Available at WHSmith, Tesco, ASDA, Borders, Eason, Sainsbury's and most bookshops*

www.silhouette.co.uk

M X0830

# 2 FREE

## BOOKS AND A SURPRISE GIFT!

We would like to take this opportunity to thank you for reading this Silhouette® book by offering you the chance to take TWO more specially selected titles from the Intrigue™ series absolutely FREE! We're also making this offer to introduce you to the benefits of the Reader Service™—

- ★ FREE home delivery
- ★ FREE gifts and competitions
- ★ FREE monthly Newsletter
- ★ Exclusive Reader Service offers
- ★ Books available before they're in the shops

Accepting these FREE books and gift places you under no obligation to buy, you may cancel at any time, even after receiving your free shipment. Simply complete your details below and return the entire page to the address below. You don't even need a stamp!

**YES!** Please send me 2 free Intrigue books and a surprise gift. I understand that unless you hear from me, I will receive 4 superb new titles every month for just £3.10 each, postage and packing free. I am under no obligation to purchase any books and may cancel my subscription at any time. The free books and gift will be mine to keep in any case.

16ZED

Ms/Mrs/Miss/Mr ..................................................Initials ...................................
BLOCK CAPITALS PLEASE

Surname ....................................................................................................................

Address ....................................................................................................................

................................................................................................................................

..........................................................................Postcode...................................

### Send this whole page to:
### UK: FREEPOST CN81, Croydon, CR9 3WZ